"Awright, you turkeys," said Fuzzy. "Pile out. It's pizza time in turkeyville."

As he threw open his door and hopped out, a rush of cold air swept into the back seat. Fuzzy thrust his hands into his pockets and strode toward the pizza parlor, muttering to himself. Bix, his slender form sheathed in faded jeans and a brown leather aviator's jacket, followed behind.

Mark and I scrambled out of the car, holding hands. The music of the jukebox was reaching out to the parking lot to greet us. Mark leaned over closer to me, and I shivered a little, partly from the chill that was blowing up under my jacket, but partly from thinking that he was going to kiss me.

Books by Janice Harrell

Puppy Love
Heavens to Bitsy
Secrets in the Garden
Killebrew's Daughter
Sugar 'n' Spice
Blue Skies and Lollipops
Birds of a Feather
With Love from Rome
Castles in Spain
A Risky Business
Starring Susy
They're Rioting in Room 32
Love and Pizza to Go

JANICE HARRELL is the eldest of five children and spent her high school years in the small, central Florida town of Ocala. She earned her B.A. at Eckerd College and her M.A. and Ph.D. from the University of Florida. For a number of years she taught English at the college level. She now lives in North Carolina with her husband and their young daughter.

JANICE HARRELL

Love and Pizza to Go

Keepsake FROM
CROSSWINDS

━━━━━━━━━━━━━━
CROSSWINDS
New York • Toronto • Sydney
Auckland • Manila

First publication November 1987

ISBN 0-373-88011-1

Copyright © 1987 by Janice Harrell

RL 5.5, IL age 11 and up

Dear Reader:

Welcome to Crosswinds! We will be publishing four books a month, written by renowned authors and rising new stars. You will note that under our Crosswinds logo we are featuring a special line called Keepsake, romantic novels that are sure to win your heart.

We hope that you will read Crosswinds books with pleasure, and that from time to time you will let us know just what you think of them. Your comments and suggestions will help us to keep Crosswinds at the top of your reading list.

Nancy Jackson

Senior Editor
CROSSWINDS

Chapter One

I used to think I was an expert on people. When we moved to Hampstead, I looked upon my new high school as a laboratory for studying human behavior. It was just a matter of polishing up my act a little, I thought, and then Freud, move over, Machiavelli, take a back seat because here comes Katy—expert on figuring people out and getting them to do what she wants. Call me a crazy optimist, but back then I thought that people made sense.

Of course, I had to admit that with all my cleverness, I hadn't been able to stop Bix from getting into fights. Bix was a friend of mine. He was also one of the best looking boys at Hampstead High. With his ash-blond hair and amber eyes he looked exactly like those guys you see in racy jeans ads. You might figure that his hobby would be standing around looking in mirrors, but, in fact, what he most loved to do was fight. When it came to fighting, he was a natural talent and the thud of a fist on a jaw was a sound dear to his heart. He got what kicks he could by creaming anybody at school who was dumb enough to come up against him. Luckily, hardly anybody was that dumb.

I had tried my best to cure Bix of fighting, but I had never really pulled it off. True, I had achieved a spell of peace when I helped get him and Celia Morrison together. Once he started carrying Celia's books to class and meeting her after flute rehearsals, he was so happy that whole weeks would go by without him wanting to haul off and sock somebody. But if I were honest with myself, I had to admit that this was no cure, just a temporary solution.

Did it make me humble that I hadn't totally reformed Bix? Nah. I looked on it as only a minor setback. I had managed to pull off other successful coups since I arrived at Hampstead High and among my friends I was known, I must modestly confess, as Katy the Mastermind. I think I can say I commanded a certain amount of respect for my sharp mind and my superior plotting powers. So, the Saturday night it all began I was feeling pretty smug. You know, that state of mind in which you totally forget to knock on wood?

The first clue I had that events were going to spin out of my control came on that cold evening when Bix, Fuzzy, Mark and I were all piled into Fuzzy's car, cruising down Lakeside. There was nothing unusual about us cruising down Lakeside. On any given Saturday night, that was what half the kids in Hampstead were doing. That particular night we were in Fuzzy's car, an old white monster with tail fins and a pair of large red dice hanging from the mirror. In the car's rear window a plastic skull nodded a greeting to passersby and the sticker on the bumper said, Eat My Dust. I felt Fuzzy's car neatly expressed his personality. He was not, to put it mildly, an intellectual.

Mark grabbed a handful of popcorn from the box wedged between us in the back seat and then held the box out to me. I shook my head. I knew it was not smart to try to keep up with Mark in eating as he was fully six-foot-two and never met a calorie he didn't like.

"Wah-hoo!" called Fuzzy, banging on the car door with his dangling arm.

Rich Wilson stopped in the northbound lane and rolled down the window of his car.

"Hey, you suckers," called Rich, raising his voice to be heard over his blaring tape player. "You going to Shorty's?"

Fuzzy shrugged. "Maybe later."

"Say, Bix," yelled Rich. "Where's Celia?"

Bix, his face darkening, leaned over Fuzzy and called, "She had to rehearse."

"A guy from Silver Lake says he's looking for you," Rich went on.

"Me?" asked Fuzzy in surprise.

"Not you, Fuzzy—Bix. Guy in '79 Pontiac."

A horn blared behind Rich. "See you," he called as he drove off.

I sank back into the plush upholstery of Fuzzy's car surrounded by the aroma of popcorn. We drove past the red-and-pink neon of Brendle's Ice Cream Parlor and the marquee of the Lakeside Twin Cinema. The holly trees of Lakeside Avenue were strung with lights that cast their glitter onto the lake across the street. On that side of the car I could see the black water reflecting dimples of white and red light. The glittery water would suddenly disappear for a moment when a car went by us, blocking my view like a camera shutter, but then would burst into twinkling an instant later when the car had passed.

In every town, I suppose, there is one place where things happen. It can be the parking lot of a mall or a beach or a fried-chicken restaurant that keeps getting closed by the health department. It could be any sort of place, really. There is only one requirement—that it draw kids to it with the magnetic force of a black hole. In our town, the place was Lakeside Avenue. Lakeside was where kids went to flirt, to snub their social inferiors, to show off their cars and to issue challenges to their enemies. It had everything—lights, action, drama, pizza. I was crazy about it.

Mark reached out in the darkness of the back seat for my hand and covered it with his own salty and buttery one. Mark and I had a sort of an understanding—a beautiful relationship based on common interests and mutual trust.

"Hey-ey," a sweet voice fluted through Fuzzy's open window. Fuzzy's ears began to turn red. When I glanced outside, I saw a sunbeam colored Volkswagen passing. That was the first I knew that Fuzzy was interested in some girl. Just another example of how cruising on Lakeside kept you up-to-date. If you weren't at Lakeside Saturday night, you missed out on half of what was going on.

"You could say hello to her, Fuzz," said Bix. "It wouldn't kill you."

Fuzzy's ears got even more red, in contrast to his yellow hair. "She knows I heard her," he said in a muffled voice.

He turned the steering wheel into a sharp right and we bumped up over a bit of curb, then inched through an alley into the lot of Feraci's Pizza. The parking lot was almost full but Fuzzy was able to squeeze his car in-between an ancient van and a motorcycle.

"Awright, you turkeys," said Fuzzy. "Pile out. It's pizza time in turkeyville."

As he threw open his door and hopped out, a rush of cold air swept into the back seat. Fuzzy thrust his hands into his pockets and strode toward the pizza parlor, muttering to himself. Bix, his slender form sheathed in faded jeans and a brown leather aviator's jacket, followed behind.

Mark and I scrambled out of the car, holding hands. The music of the jukebox was reaching out to the parking lot to greet us. Mark leaned over closer to me and I shivered a little, partly from the chill that was blowing up under my jacket but partly from thinking that he was going to kiss me.

Instead, he said, "Hey, can you come over to my house tomorrow afternoon?"

"You mean Sunday afternoon?" I asked, startled. "At your house?"

We didn't go to Mark's house much because his parents were divorced. His mother worked and she didn't like kids over there when she wasn't home. We all tended to hang out at Bix's house where Bix's mom kept a steady supply of brownies coming.

"Yeah, tomorrow," he said. "Why don't you come over and spend the afternoon? I'll teach you to play chess." We began walking toward the entrance.

"Your mother doesn't have anything planned for the afternoon?" I knew Mark's mother was a great believer in family time on the weekends.

"I guess I can have a friend over now and then, can't I?" he said.

"Is everything okay?" I asked, looking at him anxiously. We had moved inside and were going past the pizza ovens and into the main room of the pizza parlor.

"Not exactly. Look, I don't want to go into it right now. Just come over, okay? It would really help me out."

"But what's going on?" I asked.

"Katy, have I ever asked you to do something for me? Just do this, all right?"

"Bix, baby!" somebody called from a booth. "Where's Celia?"

"At rehearsal," Bix snarled.

A path instantly cleared for us in the crowded room. Nobody was stupid enough to stand in Bix's way when he was snarling. I could hear the electronic ping ping of the video games in the next room as we made our way past the salad bar.

When we found a booth, I slid over to the corner of it because Mark liked to sit on the outside where he could stretch out his long legs. Bix took the other corner and stared moodily at the window. Fuzzy was darting nervous glances around the room.

"Mark!" said a low voice practically behind us. The long face of Phoebe Hatch appeared near Mark, and I noted with a start that she had put her hand on his shoulder. The delicate pink ovals of her nails against the blue of Mark's shirt seemed to arouse my worst murderous instincts. It was all I could do to keep myself from picking up the Parmesan cheese container and banging it against her fingers. "Mark," she repeated in a low voice, "I know just how you feel."

Mark reached for a menu, thus effectively dislodging her hand, I noticed with some satisfaction. "I'm okay, Phoebe," he said. "How are you?"

"You don't want to talk about it," she said. "I understand. Believe me, I understand." She patted him on the shoulder.

I shot a hostile look at her retreating back. "What is she talking about?" I asked.

"Phoebe's mom works with my mom at the bank," said Mark. "Hey, what do you say we get a party-size pizza and split it?"

"Phoebe's mom knows your mom?" I prompted.

"Yeah," said Mark. "I guess Phoebe's got the idea that it bothers me that my mom is dating this Mulligan guy at the bank."

"Well, she certainly got the wrong idea about that," I said, observing the red blotches that were appearing as if by voodoo on Mark's neck.

"I don't think I want pizza," said Bix, staring intently at the plastic menu. "Maybe just onion rings."

It had quit surprising me that the guys never seemed to talk to each other about what was really bothering them. If you had asked Bix, he would have told you that Mark and Fuzzy were his best friends, but back when he was so miserable because Celia was refusing to speak to him, much less go out with him, I noticed that he would come over to my house and tell me how awful he felt but wouldn't say a word about it when all four of us were together. I guess this was because of some sort of weird macho code. I figured I would hear all about Mark's troubles when I went to his house the next day. Presumably that was why he wanted me to come over.

A skinny waiter took our order and after a while a waitress showed up at our booth with a tray full of food. She was energetically chewing gum. Balancing the tray on one hand, she looked us over and drawled, "Don't tell me. Let me guess." She picked up a drink and handed it to me. "Diet Pepsi," she said. Then, glancing at Mark's bulk, she handed him the pizza, "Medium pizza with mushroom, pepperoni, sausage, hamburger, anchovy and extra cheese," she announced. She gave the square carton to Fuzzy without hesitation. "Captain Bob's Fun Meal with the secret decoding ring." Then she checked the tray, looked at Bix and hazarded the guess, "Raw meat?"

Bix looked startled and the waitress said, "Sorry. I mean Coke on the rocks, and onion rings."

I had to stifle a smile. Bix's light amber eyes did have a way of picking up the light of the candle on the table and making him look like a predator ominously circling some camp fire.

As the waitress walked away with swaying hips, Bix said sourly, "Everybody's a comedian. This place is really going downhill, if you ask me."

"So Celia's at rehearsal tonight," I said, putting my finger unerringly on what had shortened his temper.

"Yeah," he said, crunching on an onion ring with his even white teeth. "The flute choir's doing some Christmas program thing and they've just started rehearsing it."

"Already?"

"Just the flute part. Later on they'll be bringing in a French horn and an oboe player from Charlotte and then they'll have extra rehearsals with those guys."

"I guess you'll be glad when all that is over," I said.

"After that, Celia's got the big audition for the State Band coming up in February," he reported morosely. "She's gotta be practicing for that."

"She's awfully ambitious," I said. "That's good."

"Yeah," said Bix. "I guess."

"Hey, Katy," said Fuzzy. "Look, there are reasons why I can't turn around, but can you tell me if this girl with a long yellow braid just came in?"

"Oh, I see her," I said, glancing in the direction of the pizza ovens. "It looks like she's with this guy in a green letter sweater."

"I wish I was dead," muttered Fuzzy.

All in all, I think it was safe to say that ours was not one of the most jolly booths in Feraci's Pizza that night. Between Fuzzy being jealous of the green letter sweater, Bix feeling neglected by Celia and Mark being upset because his mother was dating again, I was the only one in the booth who was feeling even remotely good.

I heard a voice from the jukebox singing "Hey! Won't you play—a little somebody done somebody wrong song." Funny thing, even then I didn't have a premonition. Here I was, the girl who had been a great hit at the Halloween carnival with her gypsy fortune-telling tent and still I didn't suspect that my turn for gloom was at hand.

Chapter Two

The next day I got to Mark's house late because I had to drive my little sister Caroline to a friend's house and then I had to go back for some of the Barbie doll things she had forgotten. Searching through a stuffed dresser drawer for Malibu Ken's bow tie and Crystal Barbie's iridescent slippers is not something that can be done in a trice, and it was two-thirty by the time I had finally delivered the Barbie accessories to Caroline and was pulling up into Mark's driveway.

Before I even got out of my car he was striding toward me, looking at his watch.

"I thought we said two," he said.

I got out of the car. "Mark, would you tell me what is going on? I mean, what's the difference between two and two-thirty if you're just going to teach me to play chess, right?''

"No difference," he said, running his fingers restlessly through his dark hair. "I guess I'm just a little edgy. Forget it."

It was a warm, sunny day of the sort we sometimes get in North Carolina even in November, and all the windows were open in the sun room where Mark had set up the chessboard. The room was furnished with wicker furniture and with big leafy plants that looked as if they survived by devouring passersby. Mark's mother was a plant freak and she was continually giving them fertilizer. I thought it was just possible she was overdoing it.

I could see a flicker of the TV screen in the family room off the sun room. Paige, Mark's little sister, seemed to be watching a videotape of *Mary Poppins*.

"Are you baby-sitting Paige?" I said. "I didn't see your mother's car."

"Yeah," said Mark. "I'm baby-sitting." He was arranging the chess pieces on the board with great care as if the game of his life were to be played on the board.

"You're really bothered by your mother going out with that guy, aren't you?" I asked.

"He's a jerk," said Mark.

"What's wrong with him?"

"He wears this little Rotary Club pin on his coat lapel, he roots for State, he chews every mouthful of food thirty times, he tells everybody about his solution to the problem of the national debt. A hundred-percent jerk. I hate to think how I'm going to break all this to Dad.''

"Have you heard from your dad?" I asked. I had the idea that Mark's father had been out of the picture for years. I remembered Mark saying that he wasn't sure Paige would even recognize him if he came to see them. He was out West somewhere.

"Just got a card from him," Mark said. He opened the drawer of the game table and pulled out a postcard. "Greetings from Guadalajara," it said in red letters emblazoned on a sombrero. I flipped the card over. It read: "Hi, Kids! Pixie and I ate a tortilla on the town square a couple of weeks ago. Just got out of the hospital. Dysentery's the easiest way ever to lose twenty pounds! Seriously, kids, all is well here. I'm sending your Christmas package early, but don't open it until . . . Love, Dad.''

"Who's Pixie?" I asked.

"A dog? A parrot? A monkey?" said Mark vaguely. "Heck, I don't know."

I had the feeling that Pixie was a young blonde and that the news that Mark's mother had a social life would not come as a crushing blow to the writer of the postcard. I silently handed the card to Mark and he put it back in the drawer.

I heard the sounds of a car on the gravel driveway outside and when I glanced out the big windows I saw the Metcalfs' station wagon.

"Your mom's home," I pointed out.

Mark didn't seem to hear me. "Now, the first thing you need to know is the way the pieces move," he said. "The bishop can only move diagonally, like this."

"Mark! Paige!" called Mark's mother. I could see her tall figure, dressed in pink slacks and a blazer, standing beside the station wagon. "Come out and meet your new sisters!"

I gave Mark a startled look, but he kept his gaze doggedly fixed on the chessboard. "The queen, at the other extreme, can move in any direction," he said. "As can the king. But the pawns are practically powerless." He added bitterly, "As in real life."

"Mark! Paige!" his mother called. "Come on out!"

Paige stuck a frightened face into the sun room. "They're here!" she said. "What are we going to do?"

"Nothing," said Mark. "Now, though the basic moves of chess are very simple," he went on, "the intricacies are in the strategy."

The front door was flung open and I heard Mark's mother's steps on the tile floor of the foyer. "Mark Metcalf!" she was storming. "Did you hear me?" In a moment she reached the open door to the sun room and stood there. "Oh, Katy," she said weakly. "I didn't know you were here." She gave Mark a look that expressed some of the six thousand or so things she would have had to say to him if I hadn't been there. "Mark, I expect you to go out and say hello to the Mulligan girls."

I noticed that "your new sisters" had been down-graded to "the Mulligan girls." Possibly Mark's mother had realized that this one big happy family thing was going to be a little trickier than she first supposed.

"Let them come in here," said Mark. "I'm busy."

Mark's mother looked at him in frustration.

"Can't do that, huh? Can't get them to come inside?" said Mark. "Those girls must be smarter than I thought."

I hastily reached for my car keys. "I guess I'd better be going, Mrs. Metcalf," I said. "See you later, Mark."

"You don't have to go, Katy," said Mark. "We've just got started."

"I just remembered I have to feed the cat," I said, fleeing.

On the way to my car, I saw in the station wagon a red-faced man in a business suit who seemed to be reading the riot act to two sullen blondes sitting in the back seat. One of the girls looked about thirteen and one seemed to be about my age.

I got into my car as quickly as possible and sped away. Some scenes are so grim, so entirely Gothic that they defy even my efforts to sum them up in a funny epigram. This was one of them.

I was tooling down Winchester Street as fast as the law would allow when I passed Bix heading in the direction of Mark's house. Without hesitation, I leaned on the horn. There was a squeal of brakes and

I looked back to see Bix's car stopped dead with a short trail of rubber blackening the road behind it. He jumped out of his car and trotted easily over to mine.

"What's up, Katy?" he asked, leaning on my car door. "Something wrong?"

"Just a little tip. If you were planning to go to Mark's, forget it."

"I was just going to borrow his chemistry book. Isn't he there? Hey, I thought he was supposed to be teaching you how to play chess about now."

"Did you know his mother is planning to get married again?"

"No kidding!"

"From the looks of things, the wedding will have to feature a security guard to keep the bride's son from heaving a fire bomb at the altar."

"Mark's not taking it too well, huh? I knew his mom was seeing this guy, but I didn't know it had gotten that serious."

I frowned. "I can't understand why Mark didn't mention anything about it to me before."

"Probably embarrassed," said Bix, looking away. "I think his mother and this guy have been going off together for the weekend and all."

"How on earth do you find out these things?"

He grimaced. "Anybody who hangs around the church has a ready-made intelligence service."

Bix's dad was the minister at the Church of the Good Shepherd, which didn't make Bix's life any easier. Or his father's, either, come to think of it.

I sighed. "Well, you better come over to my house and get that chemistry book."

Bix cast a look in the direction of Mark's house. "Guess I'd better," he said. "Poor old Metcalf."

When I got home, Mom was sprawled on the couch with the Sunday paper spread out all around her. "Did you know that Mark's mother was getting married?" she asked. "It's right here in the paper."

"I did hear a rumor along those lines," I said.

Bix followed me in the front door.

Mom smiled at him. For some reason, Bix was one of her favorites. Just possibly she was no more immune than younger women to his good looks. "Well, does Mark like his future stepfather?" she asked.

Bix and I looked at each other. "Not exactly," I said finally.

"These things take a period of adjustment," Mom said, placidly folding the paper.

I thought that was a classic understatement. I did not mention it to Mom, but it wasn't just that Mark didn't like his future stepfather. He hated him. I had the feeling that only the meagerness of Mark's allowance kept him from taking out one of those want ads in *Soldier of Fortune* magazine. You know, the sort of thing that reads Wanted: Reliable hit man. References required.

Mark did not talk about it much, but it was pretty clear to me that he was doing everything he could to persuade his mother she was making a terrible mistake. In spite of that, the wedding took place, as scheduled, shortly after the engagement announcement. The bride's attendants, Paige, Denise and Donna, wore red-velvet dresses. The face of the bride's son was a matching color.

"Why do you think Mark was so dead set against his mother remarrying?" I asked Bix. "Do you think this Mulligan fellow is really as bad as he says?"

Bix thought about it. "Maybe," he said.

"You'd think Mark would be happy that his mother is happy."

"Easy for us to say," he commented.

I could see that Bix was right. I had to admit that I wouldn't have liked it a bit if some stranger had moved into our house to stay, bringing his two kids along.

After the wedding we all heard plenty about Mark's troubles with his new stepfamily.

"They've moved into our house," he groaned Tuesday at the lunch table. "El Creepo gets the paper first because he doesn't like any wrinkles in it. We had to give away the cat because El Creepo is allergic. We can't have spaghetti anymore because garlic makes Denise nauseous. Well, I'll tell you, they all make me nauseous."

The next day we had a further report.

"El Creepo is disgusting," Mark said venomously. "He picks his teeth. I'm not putting you on. And he calls me 'son.' I'll wipe that smile off his face, just wait. And to top it off, Denise is always in the bathroom. A person doesn't have any privacy anymore. I'm writing my dad to see if I can go stay with him."

"Where is your dad now?" I asked.

"I'm writing General Delivery, Guadalajara," Mark said glumly.

Mark's new stepsister Denise lost no time transferring from East Side High to Hampstead High. As soon as the Mulligans moved into Mark's house, she began riding to school with Mark and me in the morning. She sat between us.

It was hard for me to see what I could do about that. When I opened the door to get in, Denise immediately scooted over close to Mark to make room for me. What could I say?

She smiled a lot, but it was hard for me to smile back. She had wavy blond hair that she caught up in a barrette on top of her head, full, damp looking lips and a figure that was all curves.

"She looks cheap," I said bitterly to Mom.

"Don't say anything like that to Mark," said Mom. "Remember she's his family now."

If so, it was a funny kind of family, I thought. Friday, when I got in the car, I noticed that Denise's arm was resting on Mark's shoulder. I was unable to stop myself from making a tiny sound of distress. It was all I could do after that to smile my usual insincere smile.

Saturday night, when Bix's car stopped at my house to pick me up, I was relieved to see that there was no sign of Denise. Bix, Celia and Fuzzy were squeezed together in the front seat and Mark was alone in the back seat. I was touched by Bix's thoughtfulness. He could just as easily have booted Fuzzy into the back seat with Mark and me. And considering how little he got to see of Celia, I wouldn't have blamed him if he had. I had the uncomfortable feeling that Bix knew about the problem I was having with Denise.

"Hi, Katy," said Celia, twisting around in her seat to greet me. It struck me that Celia was made of the same basic elements as Denise. That is, she had long, wavy blond hair and fair coloring, but unlike Denise, Celia was slender and gentle, a class act from head to toe. "I've got to get home early," she said, "I hope that's not going to throw everybody off."

"Golly, no," I said, sliding into the back seat. "It's great to see you." *Great to see you,* I was thinking, *and not Denise.*

Bix took off in his usual jet-propelled way and I was thrown against Mark, who immediately put his arm around me and began to nuzzle my neck. Astonished, I squirmed and looked at him wide-eyed.

"What's wrong?" he asked.

"Nothing," I said. "I was just surprised."

Everyone in the front seat carefully avoided looking back, which embarrassed me a lot. I smoothed the material of my skirt self-consciously. "Are we going for pizza tonight?" I asked.

"What about Shorty's?" suggested Bix.

"Or we could stop off at Brendle's," said Fuzzy.

"Ice cream, in this weather?" protested Bix.

"We'll just cruise some," said Fuzzy, leaning back until his yellow hair was pressed against the seat. "And see what we feel like doing later."

"I'll tell you when I need to be getting home," said Celia. She turned to explain to me. "I'm playing a solo in church tomorrow morning and I have to be well rested," she said. "It's a christening. The baby's parents asked me particularly."

"They pay her, too," put in Bix. "Our Celia's going pro."

"Well." Celia blushed. "It's more the honor of the thing."

"Denise plays the flute, too," said Mark.

"How do you know?" said Bix. "I didn't know you were speaking to Denise."

"She's not so bad," said Mark. "She was against this marriage thing as much as the rest of us. Yesterday, Denise and I were saying that the two of us ought to run away from home and leave the rest of them stuck with each other. Serve 'em right."

"She seems like a nice girl," I said in a faint voice.

"She's got a great sense of humor," said Mark. He moved his arm down to my waist and began squeezing me tightly while he breathed heavily in my ear.

I had a strong impulse to push him away and ask some pointed questions. Like what's going on with you and Denise?

For once the magic of the lights of Riverside Avenue didn't do anything for me. I was thinking about how Denise was sleeping in the bedroom next to

Mark's, how she was probably coming out of the bathroom every night wrapped in a skimpy towel. As the lights of the Avenue spun by outside, I began to feel claustrophobic.

"Let's get pizza," I said suddenly, as we approached Feraci's. I wasn't a bit hungry, but I would have done anything to get out of the car.

Bix glanced back at me. "Pizza it is," he said, promptly turning the car into the alley that led to Feraci's parking lot.

"Hey, I thought maybe we'd go to Shorty's tonight," said Fuzzy.

"We'll go to Shorty's next week," said Bix. "Tonight it's pizza."

Feraci's was packed with the usual mob of kids. When we walked in, the jukebox was playing "Torn Between Two Lovers." I felt like going over and kicking it.

"Bix!" cried Tommy Holloway. "Did you see that guy from Silver Lake that was looking for you? The one in the cowboy hat? He's right over there. No, wait a minute, now I don't see him. He was just here a minute ago. You must have just missed him. Hey there, Celia! I was beginning to think the two of you had broken up." Tommy laughed, but his laughter trailed off uneasily when he noticed Bix wasn't smiling.

"Anybody see an empty booth?" growled Bix, looking at Tommy with those amber eyes of his.

"We were just leaving, weren't we, Judy?" said Tommy, grabbing hastily at the check and scooting out of the booth. His bewildered companion trailed after him.

As we sat down, Mark's eyes followed Tommy and Judy on their way to the cash register. "That's some short skirt that Judy is wearing," he commented. "Nice legs." Under the table, his hand found my knee.

"I think I'll have the tossed salad," I said.

"I'll have that too," said Mark. When I looked at him in amazement, he explained, "Denise and I are going on a diet."

"You don't need to go on a diet," I cried. "You're perfect just the way you are." Mark was not exactly fat, and as for the softly rounded contour of his jaw and his nicely rounded middle, I liked him that way.

His only response to my comment was to nibble on my ear.

"Don't you wish the weekend would just go on and on?" sighed Fuzzy, oblivious that our sweet, teddy bear of a friend seemed to be turning into a sex maniac.

"The weekend can go on and on," said Mark, releasing my earlobe, "if you do what I'm going to do. Cut school on Monday. Bingo! An extra day to the weekend."

"You're going to cut school on Monday?" I said, getting for the first time a glimmer of how the friends of Dr. Jekyll must have felt.

"Yup," he said. "Denise says she does it all the time."

"No wonder Denise had to leave East Side in such a hurry," I muttered.

"I may take in a movie," said Mark largely.

"You know who goes to movies for the midweek matinees, Metcalf?" said Bix. "Guys in raincoats with two-day-old beards, that's who. Winos."

The old Mark would have laughed. This new version stiffened.

"But hey, as long as you're having fun," said Bix, shooting a glance at Mark.

We all knew that Mark was having a rough time of it since his mother had remarried, but I don't think it was clear to any of us what to do about it. He still looked the same—dark hair, soft brown eyes, size twelve shoes. But inside he seemed to be changing. The funny, easygoing bear of a guy we had all known was turning into a brooding, touchy type. It was as if he was living some strange movie script that was a cross between *Hamlet* and *The Invasion of the Body Snatchers*.

We didn't hang around Feraci's Pizza long after we had finished eating because we had to get Celia home. I, for one, wasn't sorry to be making an early evening of it. Once I got in, I firmly closed the door to my room, threw myself on my bed and lay there for quite a while looking at the dark spot on the ceiling where the roof had once leaked. It had the shape of a mushroom cloud.

Maybe it was impossible for somebody to recover when his whole life had been blown away, when strangers were living in his house and when his mother had thrown him over for a guy who picks his teeth. Maybe the Mark I had known was gone for good.

"A period of adjustment," I muttered, remembering what Mom had said. I became aware that some shreds of hope remained in my heart. Could it be that I just needed a little patience until Mark got through this trying time and then everything would be the way it used to be? I wondered glumly how long this period of adjustment thing was supposed to take.

On the calendar over my desk, December 19 was outlined with a heart shape drawn in red felt marker. December 19, date of the Christmas dance. Mark had been saying only a week or so ago that he was on the planning committee and it looked like fun so we ought to try to make it. I must have thought it sounded like fun, too, when I had come home and exuberantly circled it in red. How young, how poignantly innocent I had been back then, before Denise.

Now I wasn't at all sure I wanted to go to the silly Christmas dance. Particularly with Mark. What if he decided to take Denise along with us as a party favor or something?

Chapter Three

Mom hung up the phone. "Great-Aunt Magda died last night, Katy."

I was surprised. As far as I knew Great-Aunt Magda had always been perfectly healthy. In fact, when I was ten and our whole family came down with scarlet fever, it was Aunt Magda who had come to take care of us all because she never caught anything.

"You remember Great-Aunt Magda, don't you?" asked Mom.

"Sure, I remember her. What did she die of?"

"Of being ninety-one, I suppose," said Mom tartly. "People have a perfect right to die at ninety-one. We'll be flying down to the funeral, of course." Mom wrinkled her brow thoughtfully. "I think we'd better get a baby-sitter to come stay with Caroline. She's really too young to go to the funeral.''

I suddenly had a strong conviction that I was too young to go to the funeral, too. "I'll stay with Caroline," I said. "I'd love to. You know, me and Caroline get along just great. You won't have to worry about a thing."

"But aren't you going to go to the funeral? You were such a favorite of Aunt Magda's and I thought you always liked her."

"I did like her when she was alive. This is different. I am not into death, Mom, you know that."

In fact, I had never been to a funeral. Not even a funeral for a goldfish. While the other kids were humming "Requiem for a Goldfish," and processing in solemn splendor to the burial ground in the pine woods, while they were setting up memorial markers of crossed twigs and laying down handfuls of dandelions, I could always be found hiding in the pantry, hyperventilating.

For me, the low point of the fourth grade had been when Billy Moscovitch—of Moscovitch's Funeral Homes—got a crush on me and gave me his ballpoint pen. I was fascinated by the pen because in its top was a slender cylinder of water that contained a golden hourglass. If you turned the pen's point downward, the golden hourglass would slowly slide down in the water. If you turned the pen's point up, the hourglass would slowly move in the opposite direction. A simple matter of the law of gravity, of course, but I could sit for minutes on end watching that hourglass do its stuff. Its slow settling in the little cylinder of water had an almost hypnotic effect on me. At the same time the thing gave me the creeps. I intuitively felt that the fourth grade was a little too soon for me to start worrying about time running out on me. When I got to be ninety-one, yes. But not now. Why couldn't the Moscovitches have decorated their corporation pens with a little yellow duck?

In short, on a squeamish-about-death scale that ran one to ten, I would measure twelve. It had taken me long enough just to get used to that dumb skull in the back of Fuzzy's car, and it was plastic. A funeral I did not need.

Mom was biting her lip. "Of course, the plane tickets to Florida won't be cheap," she said. "If you really don't want to go..."

"I really don't," I said.

So they went without me. I should have been all bubbly with relief, but so far I hadn't felt very bubbly. Of course, I had something almost as grim as funerals on my mind. Denise.

Tuesday afternoon, while Mom and Dad were away at the funeral, I had to drive Caroline over to the Metcalfs to play with Paige. Mark's sister and mine were in the same third-grade class and were best friends except for when they weren't speaking to each other, which was fairly often.

When I drove up in front of the house, I could see a couple of lawn rakes leaning up against the oak tree out front. Caroline got out of the car, staggering under the weight of Barbie's complete wardrobe, and I heard giggles coming from the huge pile of leaves on the other side of the yard.

Just then, Mark's mother came to the front door and called, "Mark! Denise!"

In an explosion of leaves, Mark popped up so suddenly from the leaf pile that it was impossible to escape the impression he was acting guilty. I noticed his red sweater was covered with leaves. Denise rose with somewhat more dignity. While the two of them were dusting leaves off their clothes with their hands and laughing, Mark's mother was looking at them aghast.

I gave Mark's mother a cheerful wave. I am nothing if not a good actress. "Here we are!" I said. "Is Paige inside?"

Mark's mother came down the front steps, looking embarrassed. "Let me help you with all those things, Katy," she said.

I dumped Barbie's Corvette and Barbie's European Vacation wardrobe into her hands and got back into my car.

"Hi, Mark! Hi, Denise!" I shrieked, waving to them. They were way at the other end of the yard, but I could make out that Mark was grinning in a dumb kind of way.

Then I slammed the car door shut and sped away. I felt awful, as if my stomach had gone down too fast in an elevator.

I believed, however, that I had just had an important insight. It had been an accident that I had caught Mark and Denise tumbling in the leaves together. The person who was supposed to have come upon that scene was not me, but Mark's mother.

It wasn't that Mark liked Denise, I told myself. It was that he liked the idea of driving his mother and stepfather crazy. And one look at his mother's face had told me that he was succeeding. My guess was that Denise's father would have reacted even more violently to the scene I had just witnessed. I could imagine how he would like the idea of coming on his daughter and stepson making out in the leaf pile. He had missed this scene, but no doubt they could get an equal rise out of him by whispering sweet nothings over the laundry hamper or stealing kisses while carrying out the garbage.

When I got home, I threw myself on my bed and cried. After a while, I forced myself to stop, by saying the multiplication tables backward. I knew I had to stop crying because in a couple of hours I was going to have to go pick up Caroline and I didn't want to show up at Mark's house with swollen eyes. I had my pride.

The doorbell rang and I jumped up from the bed. A wild hope sprang up in my heart that it was Mark at the door ready to apologize and say that this had all been a terrible misunderstanding and all he and Denise had been doing in those leaves was looking for her contact lens. "Just a minute," I yelled. Running to the bathroom I hastily threw some cold water on my face, blotted it dry, and ran to the front door, blinking rapidly.

I flung the door open upon Fuzzy, who stood on the welcome mat. I don't know exactly how much my expression revealed but Fuzzy darted an anxious glance behind him as if expecting to see a monster licking his heels.

"Everything okay, Katy?" he inquired nervously.

"Of course," I sniffled. "What do you mean?"

"Dunno. Get these feelings sometimes. Probably psychic or something like that. Want to go for a drive?"

"I've just been for a drive."

"Not a drive really," he confessed. "Actually, just want to talk."

I had nothing to do for the next couple of hours but water the bed with my tears, and Fuzzy was, after all, my friend and fellow human being. I locked the door behind me and went out to get into his white monster of a car.

Soon we were speeding along Highway 43, Fuzzy's forehead knit in deep thought.

"You get some good ideas," he said. "That's why Mark calls you Katy the Mastermind."

I sighed. "Maybe I've had one or two good ideas."

"You helped Bix snag Celia, too," he said.

"Not really. Celia was already sold on Bix."

"Nope, Bix told me how you helped him out."

"Past glories," I sighed.

"What?"

"I mean, that was weeks ago."

"Fact is, I could use some help myself," said Fuzzy, turning beet red. "There's this girl. You've maybe seen her around. Long yellow braid."

I sighed again.

"You okay?" asked Fuzzy, darting an anxious look in my direction.

"Fine. I'm fine. The problem is, Fuzzy, that when it comes to affairs of the heart—"

"What?"

"Girls, I mean. Girls and boys."

"Yeah?"

"Good ideas aren't much help in that kind of situation. Clever plots aren't going to make somebody like you. They either like you or they don't."

He shot me a glance. "Are you studying too hard?"

Fuzzy had the perennial suspicion that other people's brains got addled by studying too hard. He himself was careful to take studying in very small doses.

"No, I'm not studying too hard," I said crossly.

"Can't quite put my finger on it, but you don't sound like yourself."

I sighed.

"There you go again," said Fuzzy.

"Well, I'll tell you what. I'll see if I can think up something."

He grinned. "All right!"

"I can't make any promises."

"Oh, you'll think of something," he said confidently.

I was glad to get back to the house. Fuzzy's blind faith was touching, but I had only said I would try to think of something so he would leave me alone. I couldn't even straighten out my own love life. What hope did I have of fixing up his?

On Wednesday, Mom and Dad came back from the funeral. Mom unzipped her suitcase, hung her jacket up and said, "You would have loved it, dear. All the cousins were there. We had a wonderful time. But goodness, I barely recognized Jack, he had aged so."

"Bald as an egg," put in Dad.

Mom's family, though strong on brains, were not much in the looks department and most of the cousins had the sorts of faces that are described as being "strong and full of character." I was glad I resembled Dad's side of the family, with my thick fluffy hair and my cute, characterless nose.

"Jack is Magda's executor," Mom went on. "He said that you were mentioned in the will. You'll be hearing from him."

"Money?" I asked hopefully.

"Not exactly *money*," said Mom. "Just some sort of remembrance. You were her namesake, you know."

It was true that my middle name was Magda, but I had managed to keep all but my most trusted friends from finding it out.

"I believe Jack said she had left most of her money to the Humane Society, but there were various sentimental bequests to friends and favorite nieces and nephews.''

I had hopes that my bequest would be something interesting. Aunt Magda in a long career as an Army librarian had traveled all over the world and her house had been full of goodies. I remembered tall Japanese dolls in glass cases, silver combs in their hair, dressed in ornate silk kimonos, their slender white hands raised in graceful gestures. I recalled a leather camel saddle, too, and a cedar chest full of bottles of nail polish in the lurid hues fashionable in the thirties. There had been closets of silk blouses, camel's hair suits, and hats in boxes, some with veils and feathers. Since Aunt Magda had never had children, she had no need of the sort of sensible polyester clothes and jeans that travel well from sand box to PTA meetings. Nothing but the best for her.

I felt momentarily cheered. "A legacy!" I said. "I like it. It has a good sound to it. Sort of like 'The Secret in the Old Oak' or 'The Chinese Twin Mystery.' Very interesting! I can't wait."

"Anything happen while we were gone?" asked Dad, leafing through the stack of mail.

"Nothing much," I said, trying not to think of Mark and Denise in the pile of leaves.

Just then I heard the sound of a familiar horn outside. I ran to the window and looked out. Mark's vintage Studebaker was at the curb, its finish of many coats of blue lacquer shimmering in the sunshine.

"Can't he come up and knock?" grumbled Dad.

"You know that he's kind of shy," I said, quickly pulling my jacket out of the coat closet. "So long."

I ran out to the car. Mark threw the car door open for me, smiling at me tentatively, in a way that made me forget for the moment how much I was hating him just then. He had such soft, kind eyes. That was what had appealed to me from the first, his kindness. I found myself thinking of the way he used to make me laugh.

"Want to go for a ride?" he asked.

"Sure," I said, getting in. I managed to keep myself from asking, "Where's Denise?"

"Beautiful weather, huh?" he said. "All these leaves make a fantastic show."

"Beautiful," I said in a small voice.

Mark seemed to realize that he had made a mistake in mentioning leaves because he immediately cleared his throat. "Have you been thinking about what you'll wear to the Christmas dance?" he asked.

"Oh, is that still on?"

"What are you talking about? Sure, it's still on. I told you I'm on the committee, didn't I? We've already put in the order for the poinsettias and lined up the band."

That wasn't exactly what I had meant. "Mark, how do you feel about Denise?"

"What does Denise have to do with our Christmas dance? I think she's going to the Christmas dance over at East Side."

"I'm not talking about the Christmas dance. I don't give a flip about the Christmas dance."

"What are you acting so mad about?" said Mark.

"Nothing," I said, feeling my courage ooze out of me. Why push it? Did I really want to hear him say that he was crazy about Denise? I did not. "I just figured, well, I wondered what it's like to have a stepsister your own age. Do you like Denise? How do you feel about her?"

There was a silence as Mark rounded the corner of Fairway Street and Niblick. Finally, he said, "I don't know."

I had the unpleasant feeling that was an honest answer.

"I mean," he went on, "sometimes she's a royal pain in the neck and other times I kind of like her."

"Oh."

"I just don't know. I can't tell up from down anymore. I don't know how much longer I can take it," he said. "I don't even feel like I've got a home anymore. The house isn't theirs, it isn't mine, it's nobody's house. I sit there hating them and counting how many days it is until I get to go away to college. My mother takes their side all the time. And she's always screaming at me, as if it were my fault we aren't some *Brady Bunch*-type family. She must have been living in a dreamworld if that's what she was figuring on. Honestly, if I thought I could get away with it I'd run El Creepo down with the car and toss his body in a dumpster. Sometimes I have this eerie dream that he's disappeared and that everything's back the way it used to be. I tell you, Katy, it's just you and the guys that are keeping me from going totally out of my mind.''

It did not seem quite the time to announce that my self-respect would not allow me to go to the Christmas dance with a two-timing Romeo so I didn't say anything at all. I felt terrible.

The next day, two enormous parcels arrived via UPS. "You need to sign for these," said the UPS lady when I came to the door. I signed on the narrow line, and looked at the packages curiously. I didn't remember Mom mentioning that she had ordered anything. I picked one of the boxes up, backed in the front door and parked it in the middle of the living room. Then I returned for the other box. The second box, like the first, was big, but not especially heavy.

"Mom!" I yelled.

"You don't have to yell. I'm right here," she said, coming in.

"Did you order something from the Haven Hill Crematorium?"

"Haven Hill Crematorium? I believe that's where Aunt Magda was cremated."

I hastily put the box down and backed away from it.

"There must be a letter of instruction or something here," said Mom, reaching for the drawer of her desk. She produced a pair of scissors and deftly ripped the package open with one of the blades.

Bits of white plastic foam came flying out of the carton as Mother rooted around in it, finally surfacing with a large blue urn. "Hmm," she said. "I wonder if the instructions are in the other box."

She ripped away the other box's packing tape, and began pulling out a huge mountain of dark brown fur. "Aunt Magda's mink!" she exclaimed. "Isn't it gorgeous? This must be your legacy, Katy."

I continued to edge slowly away from the blue urn. "What about that other thing?" I said, pointing a rigid finger at it.

Mom pulled a sheet of paper out of the second box. "Here's the letter of instruction," she said. "I thought so. This is from Jack. Hmm. He explains that he is mailing you Aunt Magda's mink, as per her instructions and advises you that in the summer it will need to be kept in cold storage and should be insured. Ah, yes, and he goes on to say that he is having the crematorium ship you her ashes as Magda wished for you, her favorite niece, to scatter them in the Atlantic Ocean."

I sat down at once on the piano bench because I could feel myself starting to hyperventilate. Mom was still reading the letter. "He goes on to say that you should be sure to scatter the ashes in the ocean not only because this is what Aunt Magda wished, but also because if you scattered them in the backyard they would do a lot of damage to the lawn mower. It seems there are bone shards. Isn't that typical of Jack?" said Mom. "So practical."

"I can't do it," I said flatly.

"Don't be silly, Katy," said Mom. "There's nothing to it. We'll all do it together when we go to the beach this summer." She picked up the urn very carefully, holding it with both hands. "Until then, I'll just put Aunt Magda in on your dresser."

"My dresser!"

Mom was already walking down the hall, carrying the urn. "Well, you know I've got all those stacks of sewing piled up in the master bedroom, dear, as well as those folders your father is always bringing home from work. I just don't have the space. And we certainly can't put the urn in Caroline's room. It might get broken."

I followed her down the hall, moaning softly. "Mom, why couldn't Aunt Magda get buried, like regular people?"

"Well, dear, she moved around a great deal in her work, living in all those foreign countries, and I suppose she didn't feel as if any place was really home. I recall that she always loved the sea. She traveled across the Atlantic five times, back in the days of the great ocean liners. Ah, she had a good life."

Mom placed the blue urn directly on my dresser. Its image was reflected in the mirror so the imaginative person might well feel she was being taken over by crematorium urns.

I sat down on the bed and looked at it hopelessly. "Maybe we could put it in the dining room?" I suggested.

Mom laughed. "In the middle of the dining table? Be reasonable, Katy."

"What about the living room, then? How about on an end table? Or what about the utility shed out back? That's it! The utility shed!"

"Really, Katy. I hardly want to put Aunt Magda out with the lawn mower. It doesn't seem very respectful. Now, quit worrying about it. You let yourself get entirely too wrought up about little things. I promise you, in a couple of weeks you won't even notice it's there."

Not likely, I thought, looking at it with wide eyes. I tried not to think of the ashes and bone shards inside the urn. To think that after all the long and interesting life that Aunt Magda had had, everything of her that was left was in that little jar. It was more than strange, it was creepy. I was not cut out for thinking depressing things like that. I jumped up, wondering if I could sleep on the couch from now until June.

The doorbell rang and I went to answer it. It was Fuzzy. "Here," he said, digging a bit of paper out of the rear pocket of his jeans. He carefully unfolded it and handed it to me. "Here's the information about the girl," he said. "I put down everything I could think of."

"Information?" It was hard for me to tear my mind away from Aunt Magda and back to ordinary things.

"You know, like when you get a bloodhound to go after somebody, you give it a shoe to sniff or something," he explained patiently. "I figure that if you're going to figure out a plot, you need the information. Something to go on. Do you get what I'm saying?''

"Oh, well, sure. I'll look it over."

"Thanks," said Fuzz. "I'm counting on you, Katy."

When his white car took off in a cloud of smoke, I was still staring at the creased sheet of paper.

It was at times hard to make out Fuzzy's writing because he had written all over the page at weird angles, sticking in lines and words with arrows and dots whenever he thought of something, but I thought I could make out the gist of it.

"Was B squad cheerleader. Had to drop cheerleading because of grades. Has brother named Bruce who works at Finch's Dry Cleaners. Rides school bus #57. Approx. 5'2'', 110 pounds. Name: Winkie Bowen. (Real name: Winifred.) Has pierced ears. Lives at 4026 West Haven Court. Collects stuffed animals. Is afraid of heights. Blue eyes. Wore glasses in sixth grade. Now wears contact lenses."

Awed, I realized I was holding in my hand the most sustained intellectual effort of Fuzzy's life. True, he trailed off a little and at the end had written merely, "Winkie, Winkie, Winkie" and then "Winkie Bowen Wallace" and "Mrs. Fuzzy Wallace," but still and all, it was a remarkable achievement. I wondered where he had gotten all that information.

The facts about Winkie Bowen began clicking in my mind in spite of myself. Once a plotter, always a plotter, I suppose. Contact lenses, school bus—were there any possibilities there? Couldn't I think of some cunning plot that would drive Winkie Bowen into Fuzzy's arms? But when I absentmindedly walked back to my bedroom, I was brought up short by the sight of the blue urn and Fuzzy's romantic hopes vanished from my mind. Aunt Magda! I was going to have to *do* something about Aunt Magda. I couldn't go on living like this. I couldn't cope with so many different problems at one time.

I charged into the kitchen where I found Mom chopping celery. "Mom, can't we go to the beach before summer?"

"What do you have in mind?" she asked, scraping the celery slices into a bowl.

"Like maybe this weekend?"

"Goodness, the beach will be freezing. Why ever would we want to do that?"

"Mom, I am not kidding, I just cannot take Aunt Magda's ashes for another six months. I can't take having them in the room for another day, even."

"Those ashes are perfectly harmless, Katy. Why do you have to be so squeamish?" she said in exasperation.

"Well, I happen to know you're not so crazy about going on Ferris wheels either. Everybody's got some kind of little problem. I am just not, as it happens, a death-oriented person." I shivered.

"Well, if it's that important to you," she said, scraping the celery into a bowl, "you'll just have to figure out some sort of solution. Maybe you can get one of your friends to drive over to the Outer Banks with you this weekend to take care of the ashes. It's a long drive, three hours or so, I believe, but you could do it in one day.''

"That's true," I said, brightening.

"Why don't you ask Mark if he'll drive over with you? He's a careful driver. I'd feel comfortable with that.''

I wouldn't, I thought. With things the way they were between Mark and me, the last thing I wanted to do was to ask him for a big favor.

"Driving over this weekend's a great idea," I said. "I'll ask Bix."

"Bix?" said Mom, her hand poised in midair.

"He's never had a moving violation, Mom. He's a safe driver. I think I'll call him right now." I didn't mind a bit asking Bix to help me out. He owed me one.

Chapter Four

Is that it?" asked Bix, eyeing the blue urn on my dresser.

"That's it. Could you carry it out to the car? I'd rather not touch it, to tell you the truth."

Bix grinned.

"Easy for you to laugh," I said.

As soon as Bix had taken the urn out to the car, I got Aunt Magda's coat off the heavy wooden hanger in my closet. The fur was the color of bitter chocolate and was luxuriously lined with gray satin. As soon as I slipped into it, I hurried after Bix.

Outside the sky was dark and a cold wind was blowing. I saw that Bix had put the urn on the back seat and had stuffed towels around it to keep it from rolling. "You're sure it won't tip over?" I asked, peering at it anxiously.

"Safe as houses," said Bix, then he spotted my coat. "What is that thing you've got on?"

"Mink," I said, sliding in next to him in the front seat. "Like it? Aunt Magda left it to me in her will. I thought she'd want me to wear it today."

Mom's car pulled up beside ours and she climbed out dangling a plastic gallon of milk from one hand. "I thought you kids would be long gone by now," she said. "Aren't you getting off kind of late?"

"We've got heaps of time, Mom. All we have to do is scatter the ashes and turn right around and come back."

She glanced at the urn in the back seat. "Don't go too fast, now. You be sure to drive carefully, Bix."

Bix promised to drive carefully and I waved good-bye to Mom as we backed the car out of the driveway.

"Do you have a map in the glove compartment?" I asked. I banged on the glove compartment catch but it seemed to be stuck.

"I know the way," he said. "Nothing to it, we just head east."

A bit later we found ourselves on an almost empty stretch of two-lane highway.

"I guess you're wondering why I didn't ask Mark to drive with me over to the beach," I said.

"Want to talk about it?"

"No." I sighed.

"You'd rather sigh. All right."

"I think he's going out of his mind," I said. "What do you think? I'm not just saying that because he's always making out with Denise, either. It's my objective opinion based on my careful study of human nature and my impartial observations. He's going bugs."

"Making out with Denise, huh?"

I pulled a Kleenex out of my pocketbook and blew my nose. I felt awful.

"I'll tell you what," said Bix. "I think it's got something to do with his mother getting married again."

"Of course, it does," I said with a sniffle. "If his mother hadn't married El Creepo, Denise would still be over at East Side somewhere. But what difference does it make? I can't stand this anymore."

Bix shot me a look of silent sympathy.

"Remember that time you talked me into kissing you in front of Mr. Benson's chemistry class so that Celia would be jealous?"

"Yup. You kept saying it was a bad idea. It worked, though. Up till then, Celia wouldn't give me the time of day."

I hiccuped and blew my nose. "In your case, it happened to work, I'm not denying that. But making somebody jealous is very risky. You can't tell what they might do. Like right about now, for example, I am considering joining a convent. I perceive that this is not a very practical idea since I have a feeling there are but a limited number of Methodist convents, but the idea has a definite appeal. No Denise. No boys."

"Don't join a convent, Katy," Bix said.

I could feel hot tears running down my cheeks and I hastened to blot them up before they fell on the mink. "I just don't know how much more of this I can take," I said. "I am not cut out to be a member of a harem."

"Try playing second fiddle to a flute," said Bix. "That's not much fun either."

I switched on the radio. The solid beat of "Heartbreak" hit my ears. I winced and hastily switched the channel. A ponderous voice said, "And now, live from the Coliseum, *The Magic Flute*!"

Even the airwaves were against us. I switched the radio off and glumly contemplated the fields we were passing, fields of dry stalks of corn, fields of stubby tobacco stems stripped of their leaves, mown fields with round bales of hay lined up along their edges. After a while we passed a combination gasoline station-grocery store with a sign out front saying Smith's Grocery—Drink RC Cola.

"Bix, do you think sex is really important?"

"What kind of question is that?"

"You don't have to answer if it embarrasses you."

"I'm not embarrassed. Just surprised, that's all. Well, I'd have to say in some ways yes and in some ways no. I mean, in some ways it's important and in some ways it's not."

"I'll bet if I were walking around Mark's house in a bath towel, he'd be paying me more attention," I said.

"Okay, I'll admit it—you're embarrassing me. Why don't we talk about something else, okay?"

I glanced at the speedometer. "You'd better slow down," I said. "We don't want to get a ticket."

"Sorry," he said, lightening his touch on the accelerator. "Katy, tell me something. These days, with Denise around and all, do you have this really strong urge to go out and belt somebody? You know, to sock them good and then grind their face into the dirt with your heel?"

"No, I can truthfully say that I do not," I said. "You need to work on that tendency to violence you've got. Have you ever tried crying instead of socking people?"

He shrugged. "It works for me."

The sky was so dark it looked like twilight outside though it wasn't yet noon. I banged on the catch of the glove compartment some more and this time it fell open. A brown leather glove fell to the floor. I stuffed it back in the compartment and pulled out the map of North Carolina.

"I've never heard of anybody actually having gloves in a glove compartment before," I said.

"They were in the pockets of my jacket when I got it. Kind of handy if your knuckles get all banged up. You don't like to go around looking like you've been to the wars."

I did not like to dwell on how Bix's knuckles got scraped. "Where did you get that jacket, anyway?" I asked, casting a glance at the venerable brown aviator's jacket he was wearing.

"Pawn shop. I guess some poor sucker of a flyer was down on his luck."

"Or dead," I said. "That thing must be practically an antique."

I unfolded the map across my lap. "Are we still on 97?"

"I don't know. You don't remember what that last sign said?" asked Bix.

"I thought it said 42. That's what's bothering me. It looks to me as if we should take 97, which turns into 125 and then there's this short squiggle that I can't tell what it is, maybe it's another part of 125 and then we get on 42 for four miles and then on 903 for another bit and then it connects up with 125 again and then we're on 65 and then we should be okay."

"I expect we're still on 97."

"I wish we'd see another sign," I said.

The miles went by. We passed fields, tobacco barns and an unpainted little store with a sign that said Fuller's Corners—Coca-Cola. A mist was falling and Bix turned on the windshield wipers.

"I think we'd better ask," I said. "What if we've missed the turnoff?"

"We ought to see another road sign pretty soon," said Bix.

"I think we ought to ask," I said.

"We'll be seeing a sign any minute," insisted Bix.

I was silent. After another fifteen miles, we did see a sign. It said 17. "We'd better ask," I said.

"There isn't any place to ask," he said between clenched teeth. "I'll just turn around and we'll go back to wherever we missed the turnoff."

"But what if we miss it again? We really need to know where we are. Stop right here! Here's a convenience store. We can ask here."

Bix silently drove past the gas pumps of the convenience store and pulled up near the ice machine. "This is your idea," he said. "You ask."

I drew my coat tightly around me as I stepped out into the wind. A fine misty rain was whipped into my face and I could almost feel my hair going "bo-oing" into kinks.

The sidewalk in front of the store was slick with rain and oil spots so I picked my way carefully up to the glass doors. The skies were so dark that all the store's lights were on, including the one in the window, an orange neon outline of a cigarette with neon smoke curling above it. When I stepped inside the store, I could see that at the very back of the store, near the refrigerated drinks, a fat woman in a wraparound apron was putting cans on the shelves, totally indifferent to the jingly bells on the door that had announced my entrance. A young black man wearing a broad-brimmed white fedora and sunglasses was leaning on the counter. I noticed he was wearing tight, bell-bottomed purple trousers and was chewing on a toothpick.

"Like wow, look at that thing, baby!" he said. "Hey, is it okay if I touch it?"

"Well, uh..." I said.

He began stroking my coat enthusiastically, which made me more than a little nervous since I was still in it.

"That is some beautiful coat. How much you say something like that's worth?" he asked.

"Not much," I said quickly. "It's very old. Full of moth holes and all. Actually, it's probably imitation mink. My aunt left it to me and she was very cheap, a notorious tightwad."

"Nooo," he said, holding my lapel between his thumb and forefinger. "I can tell this is real fine fur. I happen to know a little bit about fur."

A cold rush of air swooshed into my face as the glass doors of the store were thrown open and Bix grabbed my hand. "Come on, Katy," he growled. "The hounds are getting restless. You know how you hate it when they slaver all over the car."

He practically pulled me out of the store, which was a good thing because I seemed to have lost all powers of locomotion. He pushed me into the car and with a quick slamming of doors and a roaring of the engine, we were out of there.

"You had to ask," Bix said bitterly. "Nothing would do but you had to stop and ask."

"He seemed to be quite a fur fancier, didn't he?" I said.

"Did you see those bell bottoms?" said Bix. "Probably had a razor strapped to his ankle."

"No! Oh, I don't think so. I'm sure not."

"Well, I don't know about you, but the last time I saw anybody in bell bottoms was on a documentary about Woodstock."

"That doesn't have to mean anything. The man was obviously an individualist about his dress," I said.

"Quit talking to me," Bix commanded. "I'll bet I missed that turnoff back there when you started talking about sex."

"Excuse me," I said with elaborate courtesy.

The next number of miles were passed in stony silence.

Bix found the turnoff at last. It took a while, but I began to feel confident we were back on the right track when at last I saw a sign that said 64. According to the map, it was a straight shot from there on. I could relax and watch as the farm fields began to give way to coastal flats.

After a couple more hours driving, we came in sight of Albermarle Sound. The Sound was as dark as the sky and flecks of foam moved on its surface. I noticed that the few small trees that grew on the plain were bending under the wind.

"According to the map we ought to be getting there pretty soon. Roanoke Island should be straight ahead," I said.

I refolded the map, but I couldn't get the glove compartment open to put it away so I stuffed it under my seat. Presently, Roanoke Island loomed ahead of us and then, with the road slipping away swiftly under us like an unknotted thread, we left the island behind. We were driving past the site of Sir Walter Raleigh's colony, which had mysteriously disappeared four hundred years before. Not far away the Wright brothers had conducted experiments in aviation. Now it was hard to believe that history had been made around here. The scenery that passed outside our window was standard American vacationland—bait and tackle shops, ads for hang gliding and outdoor dramas, restaurants, motels.

"Okay," said Bix. "We're almost there. We're coming onto Nag's Head." After we crossed the bridge to Nag's Head, we drove past some earthmoving equipment and up to a big motel parking lot. A brightly lit restaurant stood next to the motel. Lights of motels, restaurants, and condominiums stretched as far as we could see, though I knew we must be close to the ocean because I could hear it roaring directly ahead of us. "I think this may be as close as we can get to the beach," said Bix. "I'll carry the urn."

I opened the car door, stretched my stiff legs and stepped onto the black asphalt of the parking lot. The wind whipped my hair into my face and I immediately began to feel chilled to the bone. I pulled Aunt Magda's fur coat tightly around me.

Bix pressed the urn securely against his chest as we began picking our way across the parking lot in the mist. In the light cast by the nearby restaurant I could see droplets of moisture gathering on strands of his ash-blond hair, and the leather of his brown jacket was beginning to take on a dark sheen from the dampness. It was a dark enough afternoon that every motel and restaurant along the beach had turned its lights on. Suddenly I stopped.

"What's the matter," said Bix, resting the urn on one hip so he could push his hair out of his eyes. He was squinting against the wind.

"I don't know," I said unhappily. "It's all wrong. You know, the restaurant, the bar and grill, all these motels and condominiums. It just doesn't seem right for Great-Aunt Magda's ashes. Do you see what I mean?"

Without a word, Bix began walking back to the car. I trotted after him. "You don't think I'm just being stupid, do you?"

"No, I see what you mean."

"Maybe we could drive farther down to some more undeveloped part," I suggested. I did not relish the idea of putting in over six hours of driving only to return Aunt Magda's ashes to the top of my bureau.

Bix had already opened the car door and was buttressing the urn with towels once more. "We can drive down to Okracoke," he said. "There's a stretch of protected beach down there. Not a thing on it."

"That ought to do it," I said, settling into the front seat. I pushed the buttons on the dash to get the car heater to come on and a rush of warm air hit my cold feet.

The road that skirted the beach was wet and slippery so we proceeded with caution. It took us another hour to drive down as far as Cape Hatteras where we could catch the ferry to Okracoke.

"We better get a ferry schedule," I said, as we stood by the car waiting for the ferry. "It's getting on in the afternoon and we don't want to get stuck on the island."

"Good idea," said Bix. He ran over to the white frame administration building and returned with a copy of the ferry schedule. "What we'd better do is get the ferry from the south end back to the mainland," he said. "That'll be faster than backtracking up through Nag's Head."

The ferry blew its whistle and slowly approached our shore. Then it bumped its rubber bumper against our dock and a ramp was put down for us to drive on. Only two other cars were behind us in line. It was definitely not the high season for going to the beaches and it was easy to see why. The weather could hardly have been worse. After we drove the car onto the ferry, we both got out and stood watching the gulls flying alongside of us. I could see their wings pulling against the wind but since the ferry was going at the same speed they were, they seemed to be staying still in spite of their moving wings. The only evidence that we were moving was that the shore ahead of us was growing gradually closer.

"You know, it's good to get away like this," said Bix, "the ocean, the smell of the saltwater, the boat whistle and all. It's different enough to take your mind off things."

"You're right," I said. "We ought to do this more often. Anytime we want to spend six to eight hours on the road to stand out in the cold and wet."

He laughed and leaned on the railing, looking perfectly at ease. That was Bix. He could stroll through a garbage dump and look as much at home as the resident rat. I stuck my icy hands into the pockets of my coat and shivered. The fur coat was warm, but unfortunately, it did not cover every square inch of me. I judged my nose, for example, to be turning blue.

Soon the ferry bumped up against the shore of Okracoke Island. Bix had been right, I realized, as we drove off onto the island. The north side of Okracoke was perfect, just dunes, sea oats, and a fenced area where a few shaggy Okracoke ponies were penned. They looked like ordinary ponies to me but Bix said they were descendants of old Spanish ponies and had a different number of bones in their backbones. We parked the car next to the pony corral. Then I took off my shoes and began making my way through the soft sand of the dunes out toward the ocean.

"You want me to dump the urn for you?" asked Bix, who was following a couple of steps behind me, carrying the urn.

I resisted the temptation. "No. I'm the one that's supposed to do it."

When we got up to the water, it turned out there was a kind of wax seal around the top of the urn. Bix had to take out his pocketknife to break the seal.

"I better wade out some," I said, taking the urn from him, "or the ashes are going to end up on the beach."

"Watch your step," warned Bix. "You can see it's really rough out there."

I took off the coat and handed it to him since I didn't want to get saltwater on it. But at last there was no putting it off any longer. I waded out into the cold water feeling the hard sand under my frozen toes. Once I was out far enough that the waves were almost lapping at my knees, I closed my eyes tight and up-ended the urn. When I looked, a few ashes were still falling into the water. Suddenly a wave came in that almost knocked me off my feet and the urn slipped out of my hands and fell into the water. I decided it didn't matter. The undertow was sucking it out to sea while I struggled back to the beach. I could see Bix standing there, the mink folded over one arm, waiting for me.

"All done?" he asked when I reached him.

"I feel sick," I said.

He put his arm around me. "Hey, calm down. What'd you do? Take advanced cowardice in grade school or something?"

"Definitely," I said, taking a deep breath of ocean air. After a few deep breaths, I began to feel much better. "Golly," I said. "It's over with! It's done! No blue urn on my dresser anymore. This is great." I took the fur coat from him and wrapped it around me. The wet hem of my skirt was slapping around my legs.

Back at the car, we checked the ferry schedule and decided we had plenty of time to drive to the village at the south end of the island, eat, and catch the last ferry off the island.

"My treat," I sighed happily. "Let's go someplace that has shrimp."

The rain that had been threatening all day began to come down in earnest, pelting heavy drops on the windshield. It was as if a giant had overturned a bucket on us. An incredible amount of water was washing over the car and every now and then a great gust of rain and wind would strike the car hard enough to rock it. With all the rain coming down it was hard to tell where the road ended and the sandy margins began, so we slowed to a cautious crawl.

Shortly we came to the lights of the village at the island's south end. As far as I could tell, the village seemed to be little more than a jumble of gift shops and restaurants. We couldn't make the place out very well in the rain, but we did our best to pick a restaurant that looked a little run-down in the hope it wouldn't be expensive.

When we got inside, I took off the mink and shook it vigorously. A shower of drops fell on the restaurant's worn carpet, but the coat seemed none the worse for wear. In the dash from car to the restaurant, my hair had definitely gotten wet, but I was past caring.

"Nice day for ducks," commented the waitress, leading us to a small table on the glassed-in porch. A vase of plastic flowers stood on the table. A bit later the waitress brought an electric heater, and shined it on our feet, then took our order and disappeared. The heater was definitely a more important amenity than the plastic flowers, I decided.

"You look pretty wet," I said, looking at Bix. His hair was so wet that in the dim light it looked dark.

"You don't look so dry yourself," he countered.

"At least we're warm," I said stretching my feet toward the electric heater. "Bix, you are a true friend. I won't forget this. Just to go home tonight and not to have that urn sitting on my dresser, you can't imagine how great it's going to be."

We filled ourselves with shrimp and hush puppies, paid the bill and made another dash back to the car. I had been keeping a close eye on the time since we didn't want to risk missing the last ferry.

"This is some storm," said Bix as a gust of ferocious wind rocked the car. "I wonder what that wind would clock at?" He drove the car up to the south ferry dock, only a few blocks away from the restaurant.

The rain was hitting spitefully against the metal of the car as if it bore us a grudge. Outside I could dimly make out a moving figure, at first only a faint yellow smudge but then beginning to look like a man in a yellow slicker as it approached. The man's face materialized next to us as he tapped on the car window.

Bix rolled it down a few inches and cold drops instantly pelted us.

Rain was streaming down the man's face in spite of his yellow hood. "Ferry's canceled," he said hoarsely.

"What!" I said.

"Too rough out there," he said. "They've had to cancel the last ferry."

"But what are we going to do?" I wailed.

"The Hatteras ferry is closed down, too. You'd better put up in a motel. At this time of year you won't have any trouble getting a room." He backed away from the car and began trudging toward the car behind us to give them the bad news.

"Bix, what are we going to do?" I asked in a panic.

Bix had closed the window and was turning the car around to get in the northbound lane. "You heard the man," he said. "We're going to have to stay the night. You'd better call your mom and dad."

I pulled out my wallet and began frantically counting the bills in it. The shrimp dinner had made serious inroads into my funds. "I've only got twenty dollars and forty-three cents," I said. I don't think we can get a motel room for that."

Bix reached back into his hip pocket and threw me his wallet. I counted out twenty-five dollars and ten cents. "You don't have a credit card or anything, do you?" I asked.

"Are you kidding? Preacher's kids don't run to that kind of thing."

I licked my lips. "Well, we'll just have to do with what we have. With what you've got and what I've got we have forty-five dollars. We ought to be able to get an off season room for that."

"We'd better go back to that place we ate dinner," said Bix. "It had rooms and it looked cheap. And I know the way. Finding someplace else in this rain would be no joke."

"I can't believe they canceled the ferry," I moaned. "How can they do this to us? We were so careful. We had a ferry schedule. We *checked* the ferry schedule. I can't believe this is happening."

"Look on the bright side," said Bix. "We haven't wrecked the car." Swerving to avoid a car that was straddling the center line, he added grimly, "yet."

When we got back to the place we had eaten, Bix took all the money out of both our wallets and formally handed one dollar back to me. "In case I'm swept away by a tidal wave," he explained. I could hear the wind and the surf roaring when he opened the car door so a tidal wave didn't seem beyond the realm of possibility. He ducked his head and charged out in the rain.

A few moments later he returned, his hair soaked and water streaming off his jacket. He got in, dripping puddles of water on the car floor, and handed me seventy-five cents change. "For breakfast," he said. I tucked the seventy-five cents carefully into my change purse. A breakfast costing $1.75 might not be very nourishing, but it was definitely better than nothing.

He glanced at the gas gauge. "Lucky thing the tank's full."

I began probing the cushions of the car with my fingers. "Sometimes dimes and things slip between the car cushions," I said hopefully. But obviously this was not my lucky day. All I found was a penny.

Bix was examining the key in the light of the dashboard. "We've got room 62," he said. "And it's got a phone. I asked."

Since we didn't have any luggage to carry, it was the work of a moment to drive over to room 62 and dash through the rain to its door. I flung the door open and heaved a great sigh of relief. The room had two beds. Two beds covered with molting chenille bedspreads. The small Formica table between the beds had a lamp, a Gideon Bible and a black telephone. That was the extent of the interior decoration. That was okay with me. It was reasonably clean, it was warm and dry, and it cost under forty-five dollars, which was the crucial thing.

Bix and I got towels from the bathroom and began drying our hair and blotting our clothes as best we could.

"I'd better call Mom and Dad. Collect."

"Tell them to call my parents," said Bix. "That'll save a phone call."

I dialed the operator. "If the phones to shore are out, I die," I said gloomily.

Luckily, the phones were still functioning. In no time, I was explaining the whole sorry mess to Mom. "But I keep telling you, Mom, they canceled the ferries. It's the storm. No, we're fine. We put up in a motel here. Would you call Bix's parents and tell them?" I asked, crossing my fingers. "The phone in his room isn't working."

When I hung up, Bix was still toweling his hair. "The phone in my room, huh?" he said, a glint of amusement in his eyes.

"I don't want them to worry. You wouldn't believe how worried they are already."

He began drying between his toes. "They said they'd call my parents, didn't they?"

"Sure. I feel so stupid. I can't believe this is happening to me. It is just unreal." I pounded on the bed with my fist. "The mattresses are too soft," I announced.

"So who's going to sleep?" he said.

I shot him a wary look.

"I mean, I can never sleep in motels," he added hastily.

"Listen to that wind," I said. I looked anxiously at the window curtains. Even though the windows were closed, enough wind was working its way in from around the frame to move the curtains. The wind outside sounded like a train not very far away, an ominous roaring sound. I was just as glad not to be on a ferry in all this, now that I came to think of it. It wouldn't have been much fun if Bix's car had gotten washed off the deck.

"In the old days the houses on this island had storm plugs in them," Bix said. "Like a plug in a bathtub. Then when the big storms washed over the island and flooded the houses, they could just open the plug and drain them. I think it had something to do with keeping the houses from collapsing from the suction caused by the wind, too."

I looked around but saw no sign of any storm plug in the floor of the room. I wasn't sure whether this was a good sign or bad.

"Golly, there isn't even a television. What are we going to do all evening?" I wailed, but the words were no sooner out of my mouth that I could feel myself starting to blush. There was no getting around the fact that it was a tad uncomfortable to share a motel room with a boy, even when it was someone I knew and trusted as well as I did Bix.

He had stretched out on the bed and opened the Gideon Bible.

"'I saw that under the sun the race is not to the swift nor the battle to the strong, nor bread to the wise, nor riches to the intelligent, nor favor to the man of skill; but time and chance happen to them all,'" he read.

"That is so true," I said. I took off my shoes and slid under the covers of my bed. My toes were freezing. "It really hits the nail on the head. Like look at Denise. She's not so swift and she seems to be jolly well winning the race. And it is definitely time and chance that got to us today. What bad luck! I never dreamed they stopped running the ferries in storms."

He leafed through the pages. "Here's a better one," he said. "'Man is born to trouble as the sparks fly upward.'"

"Sort of like 'you can't win for losing,' right? What's that from?"

"Job," he said solemnly, snapping the book shut.

I jumped out of the bed and began rifling the dresser drawers. "There's got to be something to do here," I said. "An old newspaper, a treasure map, a crossword puzzle. *Something*."

After five minutes of frenetic activity I found something even better than a crossword puzzle—a deck of cards.

"How about that!" I crowed. "I knew I would find something if I just kept at it. Look what I found under the bathroom sink."

"What were cards doing under the bathroom sink?" asked Bix.

"Who knows? Rejoice and be glad," I said. "Then deal."

We played three hands of rummy and two of double solitaire and then we turned in, pulling the covers up over our definitely still damp clothes and turning out the light. I don't know about Bix, but I slept like a rock. I had had a very tiring day.

Chapter Five

The next morning, we caught the first ferry off the island. As we drove onto the mainland, Bix looked mistrustfully out the car window. "Just don't let a drop of rain fall, that's all I ask," he said. "I've had it with rain." The morning skies were dreary, but no drops were falling on the windshield as yet.

"You don't find that the pitter patter of little rain drops helps you go to sleep?" I said.

"If I never hear a drop pitter or patter I'll die happy," said Bix flooring the accelerator.

My head jerked back as we took off. To travel with Bix was to court whiplash on a daily basis. "You mean you would have wanted to miss our stay in that charming motel with its quaint antebellum bed-spreads?''

"And the roaches."

"You're putting me on. There weren't any roaches."

"I didn't want to spoil your good mood," said Bix. "So I didn't mention the one I saw crawling up the curtain."

I collapsed into giggles. I don't know if I was getting punchy or what, but by then the whole thing was starting to seem funny.

When we were well out onto the highway, we pulled over at a convenience store to get breakfast. "Just one thing, Katy," Bix said before we got out. "Leave the coat in the car, will you?"

I left the coat in the car.

Inside the Mini Express Store we learned that for a dollar and seventy-five cents we could buy a small milk and two squashed rolls with their icing sticking to the cellophane wrapping. Once we paid the sales tax, we had a nickel left over for emergencies. I just hoped we didn't run into any emergencies. We were hungry and we gobbled down the buns as soon as we got back to the car. Then Bix licked every smidgen of icing off the wrapping.

When we finally got home, just before lunch, we were not so dumb as to tell the whole story of our misadventures to our parents, but the odd thing was that the more hours that passed between us and that grim Saturday, the funnier the whole thing seemed— Great-Aunt Magda's ashes, the hood with his eye on the mink coat, the ferry getting canceled, the awful motel—the whole adventure started seeming more and more ridiculous.

Monday, we were telling the guys all about it at the lunch table. "And then Katy looked like she was going to faint and the blue vase fell in the drink and headed for the coast of Spain," said Bix, choking with laughter.

"And it started to pour down, you know the forty days and forty nights sort of rain. I mean it was like life in a bucket," I went on. "And we made the mistake of having this delicious shrimp dinner, but this is where we really went wrong, we spent thirty bucks at that place."

"Ho boy," said Bix, covering his eyes. "I shouldn't have had that dessert, but anyway..."

"So we headed for the ferry, then," I explained, interrupting. "You see we had the ferry schedule and we'd checked and double-checked it."

"Katy thought she was being so careful." Bix grinned.

"And then they canceled the last ferry because the water was too rough, you see!" I put in. "And the guy says, 'you'll have to put up in a motel for the night.' I couldn't believe it."

"And we only had forty-five bucks between us, so we had to stay in this ratty motel. Katy said the bedspreads were there when Sherman passed through."

"They were molting," I said. "I'm not kidding. Weren't they Bix?"

I think Bix noticed before I did how quiet Mark had become and how white his face was because he added quickly, "Of course, all we did was play cards all night because the place didn't even have a television."

Mark reached over the table and grabbed at the neck of Bix's shirt, his teeth bared in a snarl.

I heard the shirt rip and noticed that Bix's fist was clenched. "Watch it, Metcalf," he growled. "You're getting the wrong idea about this, I'm telling you."

"I'm going to stomp your face into putty, you double-crossing—"

"Any trouble, boys?" said Mr. Fenner, his mild eyes narrowed as he looked down at us, his tray in his hands.

Mark's fingers loosened their grip on Bix's collar and his hand fell limply on the table.

"Do you have some kind of problem, Mark?" asked Mr. Fenner.

"No, sir," choked Mark.

"What about you, Bix?"

"No problem," said Bix. "Metcalf and I were just making an arrangement to get together after school."

Mr. Fenner looked troubled. He was a gentle man. "Maybe you boys would like to come by my class after school and we can talk. Clear the air."

"There's nothing to talk about, sir," said Mark. "We're fine."

"Well, if you're sure," said Mr. Fenner, moving away, but keeping them in his peripheral vision just in case.

"It'll be my pleasure to knock your block off, Bixby," whispered Mark.

"You're welcome to try," said Bix, straightening his collar.

"Mark—" I began. But he kicked his chair out from behind him and stalked away without saying another word.

I was shredding my napkin with my fingers. "You're not going to fight him, are you Bix? Surely, we can just explain."

"Of course, I'm going to fight him," said Bix. "That's what he wants. You heard him."

"He got totally the wrong idea. Fuzzy, can't you go and explain to him? He's too mad to listen to Bix and me."

"You shouldn't have told him that junk," said Fuzzy.

"*You* didn't get the wrong idea, did you, Fuzz?" I asked anxiously.

"Nope, but I'm not nutso the way Metcalf is these days. You shouldn't have told him."

"Would you quit saying that!" I cried. "The question is, what can we do now? Can't somebody reason with him? Bix, why don't you just call him up and say you won't fight him? This is crazy. You two are friends!"

"You're forgetting, Katy, he's the one that wants to fight. You expect me to let him grab me by the neck and shake me right in the middle of the cafeteria and then tell him I'm afraid to fight him?'' Bix got up abruptly and left.

Bix and Mark had been so busy making dramatic exits that they had left their scarcely touched trays right on the table. It was up to Fuzzy and me to stuff the contents of the abandoned trays onto our own trays and carry it all up to the trash bins. ''We've got to do something, Fuzzy,'' I muttered. ''Those two are crazy.''

''We better,'' he agreed. ''Bix'll kill him. Mark hasn't been in a fight since the second grade. I don't think he even knows how to fight. Not a fighting sort of fella, Mark.''

''Or Mark might kill Bix!'' I said. ''He's so big.''

''Hard to kill Bix,'' said Fuzzy thoughtfully. ''He's good.''

''All Mark would have to do is fall on him,'' I said in exasperation. ''Look at the size of his hands, his feet, think of what he weighs.''

''Maybe you're right,'' said Fuzzy finally. ''Maybe Mark will kill Bix.''

''Fuzzy! Listen to me! We don't want either of them to get killed, do we? We've got to talk them out of it, that's all. You talk to Mark, okay?''

''You're afraid to get close to him, huh?'' he said. ''You always were a smart one, Katy. Well, I'll do what I can, but what if he won't listen to me?''

''*Make* him listen to you!''

I called Bix up that night to reason with him.

''Look, I didn't start it,'' was all he would say.

"But we know Mark is sort of unglued. Don't you think you could kind of make allowances? Just say whatever you have to say to get him to back down."

"Like that I'm afraid to fight him?" he said sarcastically.

"Do you think that would work? Yes, maybe that's a good idea. Throw yourself on his mercy."

There was a click at the other end. Bix had hung up on me.

I quickly dialed him back. "Bix?"

"You must be out of your mind, Katy," he said in a strained voice.

"I'm sorry. It was just an idea. I mean, don't we all want to avoid this fight thing? That's all I was thinking of."

"I'm perfectly happy to fight Metcalf any time he wishes," said Bix coldly.

"Have you set a time? Oh, you have. I can tell you have. You've talked to him, haven't you, Bix?"

"Day after tomorrow," he admitted grudgingly. "We're going to use that vacant lot just off Lakeside."

"Oh, I'll bet it's full of broken glass and—Bix, can't you just explain to him?"

"He doubted my word," Bix said haughtily. "There's nothing else to say. I've got to go, now, Katy. I've got work to do."

After we hung up, I stared at the phone in frustration for some time. I remembered that Mark once said that Bix had the outlook of a medieval knight. It was

Mark, in fact, who had pointed out to me how inconvenient this was in the modern world, how likely it was to land you in detention, if not in jail. Back in those days, I never dreamed I'd have such an excellent occasion for seeing what Mark meant.

Wasn't there anybody who could get through to Bix? I wondered. Suddenly it hit me. Celia! He was putty in her hands. I would go over to Celia's house and ask her to intervene. I knew how she loathed the way Bix got into fights.

I grabbed the car keys and left at once. I wondered why I hadn't thought of this sooner. Celia would be able to reason with him. When I got out of the car at her house I could hear the clear, silver sounds of the flute coming from the living room. When she came to the door to greet me, she was holding the flute in one hand. "Katy!" she said, smiling at me. "Gee, I'd love to talk, but I've only got in fifteen minutes practice time so far. I had an unbelievable amount of chemistry homework. Did you need to borrow a book or something?"

"I need to talk to you," I said, edging my way in the door. "It won't take long."

I followed her into the living room. Perching on the edge of the couch near the flute stand, I explained to her about the upcoming fight.

"But I don't understand," she said, looking confused. "I thought Bix told me that Mark never fights with anybody. And Bix and Mark have been best friends forever. What are they fighting about?"

I explained briefly about Bix's and my misadventures at the Outer Banks.

She had taken the flute apart as I talked. Now she took out a cloth, attached it to a metal rod and began absentmindedly plunging it into the flute, cleaning it. "You asked Bix to go with you?"

"Well, I couldn't ask Mark because, well, things haven't been the greatest between us lately, to tell you the truth."

"You have been having troubles with Mark so you decided to ask Bix to go with you," she said, her lips growing stiff. "I understand."

"You see, I just had to get rid of those ashes," I said. "It wasn't anything personal."

"I follow you. Anyone would have done, but you picked my boyfriend." Her voice seemed to be going up a register. I had forgotten what a jealous type Celia was.

"Wait a minute," I said, frowning. "I don't think you're really following me here. You know that Bix and I are just friends. Mark jumped to the conclusion that because we didn't have enough money for two motel rooms, that there was some sort of ulterior— well, Mark is just going off the deep, that's all. There's nothing to it at all."

Celia was furiously cleaning her flute. "I'm sure Bix would not pay the slightest attention to anything I would say to him," she said. "Since you two are such good *friends*, you had better speak to him yourself."

"Oh, for pity's sake, Celia."

She was fitting the flute pieces back together and avoiding my eyes. "I really must get back to work," she said.

I was so disgusted, I got up and left without saying another word. I couldn't believe she was being so petty. Didn't she even care that Mark and Bix could really hurt each other? She was so busy being jealous she wasn't even thinking of that. If one of them ended up with a broken bone or a concussion, I thought bitterly, then she'd be sorry.

As soon as I got home, I called Fuzzy.

"Did you have any luck with Mark?" I asked him anxiously.

"Nah."

"Well, what was he like?" I asked. "How did he seem to you?"

Fuzzy hesitated. Finally, he said, "Ever been to the zoo when they feed lions?"

"Yes, yes. What are you getting at?"

"He was like that. Growls, funny scary noises."

"But he must have said *something*. He couldn't just stand there and roar the whole time you were there."

"Seemed to think everybody was trying to take everything away from him. I could make out that much. Don't think there's any point in trying again, to tell you the truth. When I went over to his house, he was out in the garage, working out."

"Working out! Mark?"

"Could hardly believe it myself, but there it is. Guess it's hit him that he's out of shape. He had a punching bag out there. Did you get anywhere with Bix?''

"No, I don't think he wants to fight Mark, but he won't back down. And when I tried to get Celia to talk to him, she got the wrong idea."

"Tell you what, Katy, you ought to quit telling people about that stuff at the beach. Anybody could get the wrong idea."

"You're right. I see that now. But you know how crazy about Celia Bix is. I never thought that she would take it that way. Oh, Fuzzy, if Bix and Mark really do fight, it's going to be all over school!" I wailed.

"Got to keep it quiet."

"You've got to talk to Mark again, Fuzzy. I can see I'm never going to get anyplace with Bix."

"Hate to say it, Katy. But ditto at my end. Waste of time."

Naturally, the way things stood between Mark and me, I wasn't going to ride to school with him anymore, so the next morning, Mom dropped me off at school and in the afternoon, I caught the school bus home. It was crowded and ten or twelve people seemed to be having a party somewhere in the back rows. A boy in the seat behind me was eating peanuts, giving off an overpowering smell of old tennis shoes. So this is how the other half lives, I thought. I had better get used to it. Not only would I not be riding to school with Mark anymore, I probably wouldn't even be speaking to him.

I felt that with all the insight I had into the human mind, I should have done a better job of foretelling the way Mark would feel about the story of the beach. It wasn't as if I didn't know what jealousy was. I had had plenty of experience with it firsthand since Denise had come into the picture.

Somehow my knowledge of human nature was misfiring. I couldn't read Mark anymore at all. I couldn't guess what was going on in his mind. He seemed to be living in a world completely beyond my imagining lately. Theoretically, I understood that he was wildly angry, but somehow his anger always caught me by surprise. I kept expecting him to react the way he had before his life had fallen apart. I was being very dense, which was not like me.

Or could it even be worse than that? Could it be that I had unconsciously encouraged Mark's jealousy, hoping it would make him realize how much he would hate to lose me? I had read enough in the works of Sigmund Freud to know that a person doesn't always know what her unconscious mind is sneaking around and doing behind her back. Was my asking Bix to drive with me to the beach merely some very sneaky work on the part of my unconscious? I hoped not. I felt bad enough just for being dense. I didn't need the guilt of having a renegade unconscious.

Suddenly my depressing thoughts were interrupted when a girl put her books down in the empty seat next to me. It was the girl with the yellow braid. I had forgotten all about her.

"Do you mind if I sit here?" she asked, raising her voice to be heard above the din. She sat down without waiting for my answer. "I'm Winkie Bowen," she announced. Because of the roar of noise coming from the back of the bus, I could barely hear her but, of course, I already knew her name. I even knew that she wore contact lenses and that her brother worked at a dry cleaners. I was well informed on Winkie Bowen thanks to Fuzzy's detective work. I noticed that she had a rather small, sweet mouth, like a doll's and a quick, breathless way of talking.

"I'm Katy Callahan," I responded. "Is it always this noisy?"

She glanced behind us. "Pretty much. I was really glad to see you get on the bus today because I've been wanting to talk to you for ages."

"You have?" I said cautiously.

"You're friends with Fuzzy, aren't you?" she asked. She grabbed my arm. "Isn't he adorable?"

"Fuzzy? You mean Fuzzy Wallace?" I blinked.

"I just love the cute way he walks. You know, the way his feet kind of skate like they're on wheels."

"He does have his own individual way of walking, I guess." It was news to me that Fuzzy could make a girl's heart go pitter patter, but I was always willing to learn.

"I think he likes me," she went on. "I'm almost sure of it. He turns red every time I get anywhere close to him. That's a good sign, don't you think? I'm pretty sure he'd like to go out with me, but boys are so funny."

"I have noticed that lately," I said a little grimly.

"It's got to look like their idea, doesn't it? What I need is a way for Fuzzy to think that he's fixed it up so that I'll go out with him. Do you follow me?"

"A plot. You need a plot."

"That's right!" she said, delighted with me. "But it's got to look like his idea. He's so shy. I just adore shy boys."

"I think I can help you out, Winkie," I said. "Leave it to me."

"I had a feeling you could," she said. "You look so smart and one time I heard somebody call you Katy the Mastermind."

I winced. I did not fill her in on my recent failures. Let the sweet child have her illusions.

Just before we got to my house we exchanged phone numbers so we could work out any fine points that came up.

Piece of cake, I thought, as I got off at my stop. This is the easiest plot I have ever had to cook up. I'll have Winkie's full cooperation as well as Fuzzy's and all I have to do is keep Fuzzy from realizing that Winkie is just as anxious for the two of them to get together as he is. I was pretty sure I saw just how it could be done. I only wished the rest of my life were so easy.

I felt very optimistic about the Fuzzy-Winkie plot, but the prospect of the fight between Bix and Mark hung over my head like doom. It was like watching two trains steaming toward a head-on collision. Nobody wants the trains to crash, not the people who are driving them or the people who are watching them, but they just chug along, the way trains do, sticking to the tracks and not having any brakes worth speaking of and the next thing you know it's *smash*.

Chapter Six

I did not particularly want to be there when Bix and Mark fought, but I didn't see any way out of it. I figured Fuzzy and I were going to have to stand by in case ambulance service was needed.

I remembered reading that in the old days the first duty of the seconds in a duel was to try to effect a reconciliation between the parties who are trying to kill each other. If so, I'm sure no seconds ever tried harder at it than Fuzzy and me. But Bix completely refused to discuss the matter and according to Fuzzy, all he got from Mark were angry glares and inarticulate growls. As for Celia, any time you went by her house you could hear her fluting away, but as for communication with Bix, she might as well have been in Calcutta. There seemed no hope of help from anywhere. It did not look good.

The fight was scheduled for four o'clock on the lot at the corner of Trembull Street and Lakeside Court. I got there early to check around for broken glass but all I found, outside of gum wrappers, were a couple of smashed aluminum cans, which I, like a good citizen, removed. The weeds on the lot had been mown in the recent past and were now dry and crisp so there was a good surface for combat. The sky was overcast and there was just a faint coolness in the air. If I hadn't been so attached to both of the combatants I would have said conditions were ideal for the battle.

Fuzzy drove up shortly after me and got out of his car wearing an old red sweatshirt. He looked so depressed I longed to tell him about how Winkie was keen on him just to cheer him up, but I knew that for his own good I had to keep her part in my upcoming plot quiet.

"They aren't here yet, huh? Maybe they've got the time mixed up," he said, brightening.

"I hope so," I said. I buttoned my sweater up and nervously smoothed my hair. Fights were not my amusement of choice. Particularly fights between people I liked. And most particularly fights that made me feel guilty. On the whole, I would rather have been in Philadelphia.

Just then Mark's blue Studebaker pulled up on the north side of the lot and, as if operated by the same clockwork mechanism, Bix's car pulled up simultaneously on the south side. They both got out and began walking over to where Fuzzy and I stood, near the sidewalk. Mark was in tight jeans and a form-fitting T-shirt that showed the roundness of his tummy. He looked very big and although he was pale, his jaw was clenched with determination.

Fuzzy glanced at him approvingly. "Doesn't want to give Bix anything to grab hold of," he murmured. "That's why he's wearing those tight clothes."

Bix, too, was wearing tight jeans and a knit shirt, but with a better aesthetic effect since he had the build for it. He carried the brown aviator's jacket slung over one shoulder and looked unusually subdued considering that he was about to engage in his favorite extracurricular activity. I sensed that his problem was that he was not really angry at Mark.

As the two combatants walked toward each other with long, slow steps, Fuzzy mumbled, "I swear, looks like *Gunfight at the O.K. Corral.*"

Finally Bix and Mark were almost within hitting distance of each other. They eyed each other warily.

"I don't see what you're doing here, Katy," Mark said to me. "This doesn't have anything to do with you."

That remark left me speechless.

Even though I could see the telltale red splotches on Mark's neck showing that he was really mad, I could hardly believe they were actually going to hit each other. They were practically blood brothers. They had been friends since they were little kids. They would have stuck up for each other against anybody else in the world. This was one fight that didn't make any sense.

"Ready?" Mark snarled.

"Sure," said Bix, tossing his jacket aside.

All of a sudden, Mark's hamlike fist shot out to Bix's chin and knocked him flat. Fuzzy and I stood there with our mouths open, looking at Bix sitting on the ground. "Je-rusalum!" whispered Fuzzy. Bix was leaning back on his hands. His face was white, his eyes were narrowed, and there was a red mark on his chin.

"Get up," growled Mark.

Bix sprang up in a single motion, like a panther, and drove his fist into Mark's stomach with his whole weight behind it, throwing Mark off balance. Then he batted at the side of Mark's head with his left fist, stunning him, and followed it up with a quick sock to the jaw with his right.

I lifted my hand to my mouth, appalled.

Mark had sunk to his knees, but immediately began struggling up, looking a little woozy. Bix was standing off from him a couple of feet with his fists up, breathing heavily. A damp strand of his fair hair clung to his forehead.

Mark got to his feet but made no move toward Bix. He didn't even raise his fist. There was a look on his face that I couldn't quite fathom and I began to have this sick fear that he had a concussion. Then he bit his lip and said, in a slightly puzzled voice, "I think I could hit you again, Bix."

"Try it," spat Bix.

Mark raised his hand and Bix tensed, ready to strike out, but it turned out Mark was only scratching his nose.

Mark cleared his throat. "I don't want to hit you," he said. "I'm sorry we ever got into this mess."

I could see a confused look in Bix's amber eyes. If he hadn't been mad to start with, he was certainly mad now and it was hard for him to switch gears.

"Didn't you hear me?" asked Mark. "I said I'm sorry."

He held out his hand and Bix looked at it suspiciously for a full thirty seconds before he could bring himself to shake it. I think he half suspected the offered hand was some judo trick or something. His eyes were still burning with rage and I could see that he had to force himself to go through the motions of shaking hands.

Then Mark turned his back on Bix, stuck his hands in his pockets and began slumping back to his car. I was distressed to see that his lip was bleeding and that the blood was beginning to trickle down his chin. Fuzzy and I stood frozen as he walked away, afraid to say a word for fear the fight would start up again. But after watching Mark a minute, Bix bent to pick up his jacket. Then he ran his fingers through his hair, managed a travesty of a smile and ran to catch up with Mark. "Hey, Metcalf," he said in a choked voice. "You want to go get something to eat?"

I melted against Fuzzy in sheer relief. Right at that moment, I appreciated Bix, I think, more than I ever had before. I knew how easy it was for him to keep hitting and how hard it was for him to stop. I was deeply grateful the whole thing was over.

A minute later Rich Wilson pulled up his car next to mine. "Julie said there was a fight going on over here," he called. "Hey, Fuzzy, you aren't fighting with girls these days are you?"

"Get lost, Rich," said Fuzzy, opening his car door.

"No, all kidding aside, Fuzz, I heard Bix was over here fighting. Julie said it was Mark he was fighting with, but I told her she had got it all wrong. Who was the poor patsy he sucked into it?"

"No fight, Rich," I said, getting into my car. "Just an unfounded rumor."

"So what are you two doing over here if there hasn't been any fight, then?" he shot back.

I gave him a friendly smile and pretended not to hear him as I switched on the ignition and pulled out of my parking place. I wondered who else had seen what had happened and how long it would take it to get all over school.

I suppose one of the oddest features of the fight was that I didn't have any of the gratifying feelings a girl expects to have when two boys have been fighting over her. Not even now that it was all over and no one seemed to be hurt. I think I realized that there was some truth in what Mark had said—"This doesn't have anything to do with you." It didn't, really. Mark was burning with rage about the way his life had gone bust and Bix had his pride to consider. That was what the fight was about. Not about me.

I drove home full of sad thoughts. Did Mark like me at all anymore? I didn't think so. He had too many confusing things on his mind to have any energy left for liking me. He didn't want me fooling around with Bix, sure, but that was just because, as he had said to Fuzzy, my leaving him seemed like part of a disturbing trend. He felt as if everyone were deserting him.

And what about me? Did I still like him? A tough question. I did, I decided, but the way you like someone you met on vacation whom you never see anymore. As far as I was concerned, Mark might as well be living in another state. I heaved a sigh and drove slowly home.

I was surprised, when I got there, to see that Fuzzy's car was parked in front of the house and that he was leaning on it, waiting for me.

"What took you so long?" he asked.

"I was thinking," I said with dignity, naming an activity with which Fuzzy was not overfamiliar.

"What about that Rich, huh? I felt like socking him."

"Give me a break, Fuzzy," I cried. "No more socking."

"Bunch of vultures," said Fuzzy darkly. "Circling around, hoping they'll see somebody get beat up. I can't stand that crowd."

"It could have been worse. They could have seen somebody getting beat up."

"Yeah," said Fuzzy, brightening. "It went pretty good, all things considered, huh? I mean, no bones broken, no hard feelings."

"So, is that what you came over to talk about?"

"Actually, no," he said, reddening. "Just wondered how you were coming along with that plot you promised me. Any ideas, yet?"

"Fuzzy, your troubles are over. Your immediate troubles, anyway," I amended. My own recent experiences led me to think that catching the interest of one's beloved could be only the very beginning of one's troubles. "I think I have an idea. Have you seen the signs up about the field trip to city hall?"

"Yeah, boring. All the ninth grade civics classes have to go."

"And other people can sign up if they are interested."

"Who would be interested?"

"You, me, and Winkie Bowen."

"Winkie is interested in civics?" asked Fuzzy, looking badly shaken.

"I talked her into it," I said. "Now that I'm riding the bus back and forth from school, I've started sitting with Winkie sometimes."

"Good idea," said Fuzzy, rapt with attention.

"And I pointed out to her that after a tour of the police station and the new city hall, all participants would have lunch at the Eye of the Needle restaurant on the top floor. She thought it sounded like fun. Plus you do get excused from all of your Thursday morning classes. That part appealed to her."

"Yeah, I hadn't thought of that. But what good does that do us?"

"You remember you told me that Winkie is afraid of heights?"

"Yeah. She couldn't even get on the top of the human pyramid in cheerleading somebody told me."

"Well, the Eye of the Needle restaurant is very high up. And the observation deck on the roof is even higher."

"So why would she want to go there?"

"I persuaded her, that's why," I said tartly. I hadn't counted on Fuzzy asking difficult questions. "I told her it would be better to confront her fear. Do you follow me?"

"So far. Don't see what you're getting at though."

"Well, first let me tell you about this scientific experiment I read about." I was not making this up. I truly had read about this scientific experiment, and I did my best to explain it to him. "You see, they had these men walk across a bridge to reach a pretty woman. Follow me so far?"

"Yeah," he said, his brow wrinkled. "Bridge, pretty girl. Got you."

"Half of the men walked across a short sturdy bridge to get to the woman, and half walked across a long, swaying bridge to get to her."

"Sounds crazy to me. Why didn't they all walk across the short bridge?"

"Because it was an experiment, that's why. Some of them had to walk across the long bridge for the experiment."

"Oh."

"Now most of the men who walked across the long, rickety bridge to get to the woman asked for her phone number, but the men who walked across the short bridge did not ask for her phone number. Do you know why?"

"I give up. Why?"

"Because when the men who walked across the long swaying bridge got to the woman, their hearts were pounding and their pulses were racing with fear. But they thought their hearts were pounding because the woman was so pretty. Do you follow me? These guys couldn't tell the difference between attraction and fear."

"They sound pretty dumb to me."

"This was a scientific experiment, Fuzzy," I said in an intimidating voice. "Anyway, doesn't your heart pound when you get close to Winkie?"

"Sure does," he said, gulping.

"Well, there you are. All we have to do is get the two of you together up on that observation deck and her heart will be pounding like mad. Then you ask her out and she'll say yes because she'll think there is this strong magnetic attraction between you. See what I mean?"

"What happens when we come down, though?" asked Fuzzy, wrinkling his brow.

"She may still be convinced she's bananas about you. We'll just have to see what happens."

"Sounds good," said Fuzzy, lighting up. "I like the part about where she's bananas about me."

"Leave it to me. I've got a few little details to work out yet but what you have to remember is to be sure to sign up for that field trip."

"Right-o," said Fuzzy, glowing with pleasure.

It was nice to know that at least somebody was happy.

Chapter Seven

Bix?" I asked tentatively. "Have you talked to Celia lately?"

"Nah, what's the use? I already know she's booked up all weekend. Rehearsal Friday night, flute choir Christmas party Saturday night, church solo Sunday. I'll probably give her a call tomorrow and beg her to fit me in next weekend. Why?" he asked, prodding his ice cream with the spoon.

"Just wondered," I said, lowering my eyes.

I had run into Bix out at the mall and we had decided to take a break from our Christmas shopping to have ice cream. But the minute we had sat down at one of the little white tables in Vinnie's, my conscience had begun throbbing painfully. I realized that Bix did not know what I had let slip to Celia about our ridiculous adventure at the beach. When he next saw her, he would be astonished to find her gnashing her teeth with jealousy.

"I guess you're thinking Celia's already heard about the fight," he said, fingering the Band-Aid on his chin. "She probably has. I saw Julie Mason's car go by on Trembull and she's got the biggest mouth in Hampstead. Oh, well, you know what they say—man is born to trouble as the sparks fly upward." With this he managed a grin.

I realized I should warn Bix that Celia was upset about more than the fight, but I couldn't bring myself to do it just yet. I was not feeling quite strong enough to have yet another person mad at me.

"Did you and Mark have a good talk after the uh—"

"Fight," he supplied, taking a bite of ice cream. "Yeah, well, we didn't say much. Just kidded around some. Metcalf's never going to let me forget it that he floored me."

"You didn't think he was going to hit you, did you?"

He looked at me under his lashes. "How'd you guess? I kept thinking that next he was going to laugh and we'd forget the whole thing."

"He's not doing much laughing lately," I said sadly. "Do you think he believes your story about the beach?"

Bix shrugged.

"Well, he doesn't seem to be still mad, does he?" I pointed out. "Doesn't that sound as if he calmed down and saw there wasn't anything to be upset about?"

"I don't know if he believes me or not, Katy. What I think is—he doesn't care."

"Ouch," I winced.

Bix studiously applied himself to his ice cream.

"I'd rather know," I said. "Yes, I would definitely rather know. So tell me, what do you think of East Carolina's chances against Miami?"

"All I mean is, he's just not his old self." Bix said.

"I've noticed that," I said bleakly.

Bix gave me a crooked smile. "Trust me. Life goes on."

I thought Bix was in a poor position to be preaching. Back when Celia wouldn't give him the time of day, his groans could have been heard from here to Schenectady and any able-bodied male who crossed his path was apt to get his teeth rearranged. Life goes on, my foot.

Out of the corner of my eye I saw a thatch of mustard-colored hair gliding up to the ice-cream counter. Before I could turn to wave, Fuzzy called out to us and a moment later he brought his ice cream over to our table. He turned a chair around and straddled it, licking his chocolate cone.

"How about running into you here!" he exclaimed.

Then he looked anxiously back and forth between us. "I'm not butting in on anything, am I?" he asked. "Because I can just buzz off if I am."

"Don't you start!" I said. "Fuzzy, you know this isn't some private tête-à-tête."

"Tête-à what?" he said blankly. "Oh, sorry. It's just that I was down at the fountain a minute ago and Julie was talking to Sally about how Bix and Mark were fighting over this girl."

I covered my eyes. "Fuzzy you were right there at the fight. You know all about what happened."

"You're right," he said, looking puzzled. "Guess it was just, you know, when somebody says something and—"

"The power of suggestion?" I said.

"Right. Well, what do you guys give me for East Carolina's chances against Miami, huh?"

Bix and I grinned at each other.

"What'd I say?" asked Fuzzy, aggrieved.

When Bix and Fuzzy had disposed of the question of East Carolina's chances—zilch—I asked Fuzzy if he had signed up for the field trip to city hall and he assured me, with great seriousness, that he had.

"What's this about the trip to city hall?" asked Bix. "Is there something going on here I don't know about?"

Fuzzy punched him in the arm. "Katy's gonna get me all fixed up right and tight with my girl, just like she did with you and Celia," he crowed. "It's all based on—what do you call it, Katy?"

"Scientific experiments," I put in.

"Yeah," said Fuzzy.

Bix pawed disconsolately at his ice cream. "I hate to tell you, Fuzz," he said, "but your troubles might be just starting."

"What a bunch of gloom and doom, you two," protested Fuzzy.

"Don't worry, Fuzz," I said. "This thing with you and Winkie is going to be just fine. I have a very good feeling about it."

"Winkie?" said Bix derisively. "Is that a name? Winkie?"

"Watch it, Bix," said Fuzzy, lowering his brows. "You happen to be talking about the woman I love."

I could see a memory flash across Bix's face like heat lightning in a summer night. To give him credit, he realized at once that he had overstepped the bounds and apologized to Fuzzy most handsomely.

Just then, Mark came in and got a diet cola up at the counter. Catching sight of us, as soon as he picked up his cola he began moving rather uncertainly toward us. Bix quickly snagged an extra chair from the next table and pulled it out for him. In other days, I reflected, we might have kidded Mark about that diet cola, but no more. I noted with some distress the faint yellow bruise beginning at the hairline near his left ear. A couple of Band-Aids covered the worst of the damage to his jaw.

"Mob scene out here tonight," Mark offered, as he sat down heavily in the chair. He turned bewildered eyes on me and I tried my best to smile.

"Gets worse every year," Bix concurred.

"I seemed to be causing some sort of sensation when I passed the fountain," Mark said. "My hair hasn't turned green, has it?"

"Nah," said Bix, grinning. "Your fame as the dude who decked me has gone before you. That's all."

Mark smiled uncertainly. "Well, I'm glad it's not green hair," he said, running his palm over his head.

I wondered how long it would take for us all to feel easy with each other again.

I cleared my throat. "Getting a start on your Christmas shopping?" I asked.

"Oh, well, you know," he said. "Anything to get out of the house." He cast his eyes around the ice-cream shop in a hopeless way, as if he already knew that whatever he was looking for wasn't there. Finally he forced his attention back to us. "Well, what do you say we do some cruising this weekend, huh?" he said.

We all chimed in fractionally too soon. "Yeah." "Great." "Terrific idea." Then there was an awkward silence.

"Fuzzy's giving four-to-one odds against East Carolina," Bix put in.

"No takers, I guess," said Mark.

I found myself feeling desperately grateful that there was something we could all talk about without choking.

High-pitched laughter broke over the ice cream shop as Julie Mason and her friends poured into the shop and converged at the counter. I was uncomfortably conscious of a good deal of whispering when they caught sight of us all sitting at the little table together.

Mark seemed to sense what was happening because he mechanically reached across the table and covered my hand with his own.

"Smile, Katy," Bix prompted me softly.

I smiled. I supposed I resembled the skull in the rear window of Fuzzy's car because I felt awful.

"So what's it to anybody," Mark said quietly, "if Bix and I decide to have a little sparring practice, right?"

Beads of sweat were forming on Fuzzy's upper lip. "I hate this kind of junk," he said. "Jeez, what a bunch of vultures those girls are."

"Hi, Bix!" squealed Sally, as she picked up her ice-cream float.

I heard one of the girls say in a carrying whisper, "Those eyes, that bod of his—I die!"

Bix muttered darkly, "Ever feel like putting a napkin over your head?"

"Lately," said Mark, smiling at him, "lately, a lot."

One thing was clear. Mark did not want the story of the cause of the fight spread all over school. None of us did. And Celia spent all her time working and practicing the flute so it wasn't likely she'd be spreading the story. I began to feel mildly optimistic that we could slowly kill the gossip. I did not look forward to presenting a cheerful face to the world while my heart was getting kicked around daily like a football, but I figured I could do anything I had to do, to keep Sally and Julie from enjoying a good laugh at my love life. Under the circumstances, I couldn't help reflecting that it would have been better if Mark and Bix hadn't been wearing matching Band-Aids.

Fortunately for my mental health, not everything in my life was a mess. The day after the touchy scene at the ice-cream shop, a school bus took all the field trippies to city hall and this time I knew things had to go my way.

During the time we spent at city hall, I found out more than I ever wanted to know about the workings of the city government, but I was resigned to that. All around me, ninth graders were punching one another and giggling. Just a few sophomores and juniors had signed up and three of them were known juvenile delinquents who would have done anything to get out of class. Fuzzy, Winkie and I, naturally, felt kind of conspicuous. Winkie pretended to be fascinated with everything our guides had to say about the workings of the city, while Fuzzy kept hanging back, trailing the group and trying to stay out of sight. I, Katy the Mastermind, was calm, cool, on top of things. This was one operation I was sure would go on greased wheels.

After being shown endless examples of the city's peerless efficiency, at last our group was allowed to move to the top floor of the building for the scheduled buffet lunch. Knowing that I had an absolutely fail-safe plot lined up, I was able to sit down and eat my lunch with a hearty appetite. Winkie, however, was showing signs of stress. I noticed her salting her apple pie.

"Finished?" I asked brightly. "I'm finished, too." I pushed away my food. "Why don't we take a look at the city from the observation deck now?"

Winkie paled a little. This kid truly was afraid of heights. All you had to do was mention some high-up place and she changed color. Now that I thought about it, I realized she must be very gone on Fuzzy to have agreed to my plan in the first place.

"Nothing to it," I murmured as we rose from the table. "Four-and-a-half-foot guard rail, I promise you, Winkie. You'll be fine."

We moved quietly out of the restaurant toward the elevator. Just as I had figured, the teachers who were supervising the field trip had their hands full subduing the ninth graders who kept pelting each other with dinner rolls. No one paid any attention when we got up and left.

As I had arranged, Fuzzy was standing at the elevator waiting for us. He was grinning in his usual goofy way and scuffing the carpet with one shoe.

"Fuzzy!" I exclaimed, doing my best to look surprised to see him. "Winkie, you know Fuzzy don't you? Gee, so you came on this trip, too. Wasn't that stuff about how much paper they use in a week incredible?''

Fuzzy's ears began to redden. Winkie's eyes were fixed modestly on her shoes. It was left to me, as the only rational member of our trio, to press the button to call the elevator.

''Winkie and I thought we'd just take a look from the observation deck before we left,'' I explained. ''She's a little afraid of heights, but I've told her that the best thing to do with these phobias is to confront them boldly and overcome them. Don't you think I'm right, Fuzz?''

He seemed incapable of speaking and just gulped. Slowly the elevator light moved from three to seven and the doors began to open. Fuzzy stepped in and Winkie followed, her eyes still keeping a close watch on the toes of her shoes. I slapped my hand to one eye. ''Oh, dear!'' I exclaimed. ''My contact lens has slipped.''

The doors of the elevator were beginning to close. Winkie took a step toward me but I waved her back. ''You go on. I don't want you to miss seeing the view. Fuzzy, you'll take care of Winkie, for me, won't you?''

He was still nodding vigorously when the doors of the elevator slid shut. I watched with satisfaction as the indicator light moved from 7 to R. Then I sat down on the vinyl bench next to a sandfilled ash tray, and began filing my nails.

A moment later I became aware that ninth graders were beginning to surge out of the restaurant. One of the juvenile delinquents passed me with the pockets of his jacket bulging, walking off with the silverware, no doubt. The trippies were evidently preparing to depart from city hall and board the school bus for the return to school. I continued to file my nails. A mastermind is never flustered by minor scheduling difficulties. If the group left without us, we could always take a taxi back to school.

"Let's keep our voices down, please," a harassed teacher shouted over the hubbub. "Quiet, please."

Both elevators had to be pressed into service for the ferrying of ninth graders from the seventh floor back to the ground floor. It looked as if Winkie and Fuzzy might be stuck up there on the roof for some time, I reflected with satisfaction.

But at last the final ninth grader had been ferried to the floors below and I saw the elevator indicator rise from 1 all the way to R and hesitate there. A moment later, Fuzzy and Winkie stepped off the elevator together, holding hands.

"Some view, right?" I said, rising and stashing my fingernail file in my purse. "Now we'd better hurry downstairs or they're going to get away without us."

We all got back in the elevator. This time, they were both blushing and it was perfectly obvious that the conversation, such as it was, would be up to me. I turned to face the elevator doors as we went down.

"Yes," I said, "I think it's definitely better to confront your fears. You can't let these things get a hold on you. Next thing you know, Winkie, you'll be going up on mountains, Ferris wheels, the Empire State Building, rockets to the moon, hang gliding—the sky's the limit."

"Brrrrr," shuddered Winkie behind me. Then I heard a wet smacking sound. I tactfully did not turn around to investigate.

The doors to the elevator opened on the mob of ninth graders that thronged the ground floor lobby of city hall. They were now beginning to line up for the school buses. I took my place in line with the satisfaction of knowing my mission was accomplished.

When we got back to school, I went by my locker to pick up my books and ran into Bix there. "Is something wrong?" I asked when I got a look at his face.

"You might say that," he said, frowning. "Celia's got some crazy idea you and I were carrying on at the beach."

"I'm sorry, Bix," I chimed in guiltily. "I told her all about the fight when Fuzzy and I were trying to get you two to call it off. I was hoping she would talk you out of it. But when I explained about the beach, she seemed to take it all wrong."

He brushed my apology aside. "Let's face it," he said, "all kinds of crazy stories are probably going around school. She'd have heard it somewhere. But look, you told her what really happened, didn't you?

Well, so did I. And she doesn't believe me! I mean, she doesn't say much, but it's plain she thinks I'm lying. Me! Lying! Have you ever known me to tell a lie?''

The bell went off a few yards from us, probably doing permanent damage to our ear drums. Bix smiled ruefully and then took off running for class.

I was late for algebra, obviously. But that was the least of my troubles. I was suffering from a heavy dose of guilt. If I hadn't asked Bix to help me out with my ashes problem, none of this would have happened.

When I came out of fifth period fifty minutes later, Fuzzy was waiting for me. He grabbed my hand so we wouldn't be separated by the surging masses of kids that stampeded through the hall at the class change. "You did it, Katy," he said, his face glowing. "Winkie and me are in love."

"Quick work," I commented. "Congratulations."

We were moving along as we talked, trying to keep pace with the traffic so as to avoid being trampled. "It was like this," he said. "When we got up there, I said maybe we should put a quarter in the telescope so we could see better. And she looked over the edge of the railing, sort of turned white, and said she could see well enough as it was. Then she keeled over! She fainted!"

I blinked. "She fainted?" That had not been a part of the script.

"I caught her," he said lyrically. "There she was in my arms, white as a golf ball, poor little thing."

"Get a move on," growled a Neanderthal type behind us.

Fuzzy squeezed closer to me to let the cave man by.
"And then her eyes sort of fluttered and she came to
and there we were! She was embarrassed, of course,
but I said she'd better hold my hand until we got on
the elevator and then she looked at me with those
gorgeous blue eyes and I kissed her!"

A squeal of protest was heard from a girl whose foot
Fuzzy had stepped on while recounting his story but
he paid no mind. "Then I asked her for her phone
number," he said, with satisfaction. "We're going out
Saturday. I'll never forget this, Katy. You've saved my
life. Hey, here's my class." He began the tricky business of tacking across the traffic to reach the door of
his class and soon his mustard-colored hair disappeared from my view.

I should put up a shingle, I thought with satisfaction. Love life fixed, mended, or rebuilt. I was that
good. But then I recalled that Winkie had already been
seriously attracted to Fuzzy before I started so not that
much of the credit was mine. It was hard to understand how she could be that gaga about Fuzzy, but if
there was one thing I was starting to be convinced of,
it was that there is no accounting for feelings. Why
should Celia be crazy with jealousy when Bix was obviously devoted to her? Why should Mark want to fool

around with Denise when he could have charming, intelligent, attractive me? Why? Nothing seemed to make sense.

Chapter Eight

Saturday night we all went cruising down Lakeside in Fuzzy's white monster. Winkie's head was resting contentedly on Fuzzy's shoulder. In the back seat, I sat with an uneasy heart between Mark and Bix.

Bix was staring moodily out the window at the lights of Feraci's Pizza Parlor as we slowly cruised by, I examined my neatly filed nails, and Mark surveyed the lake. No one spoke.

A car with its tape deck turned to atomic blast level pulled abreast of us.

"Say, Mark," its driver yelled. "I heard a rumor you were dead!"

Mark rolled his window down. "An exaggeration, Tony. I still manage a little shallow breathing."

"Jeez, the things you hear," said Tony in a disgusted voice, "you wouldn't hardly believe. Gonna make it to the game tonight?"

Mark's reply was drowned out by the blare of a large horn behind Tony. Casting an anxious glance at the big Ford Galaxy up against his bumper, Tony instantly scooted his little Renault ahead and we cruised on.

"The Christmas decorations are so pretty," sighed Winkie.

Lakeside Drive was in full holiday rigging with a string of red and green lights running the length of the street and bunches of evergreens tied to the corner street signs with red velvet ribbon. The length of gold lamé swagged across the window of Burton's Furniture caught the red and green lights of the street and bounced them back, mellowed, from its golden depths. On the north side of the street, the lake looked as if it were tricked out in green and white sequins.

"Bah, humbug," said Mark, folding his arms. I didn't think he was kidding.

"What do you say we get something to eat?" said Fuzzy.

"I'm starving," agreed Winkie readily.

"Let's take a vote," said Fuzzy.

"I vote for pizza. I love pizza," said Winkie.

"That sounds good," said Fuzzy, promptly abandoning all pretense of democracy. He swung the car around the corner in order to circle the block and get back to Feraci's.

"Fuzzy!" yelled a bunch of boys in a Jeep. "Who's that you've got with you tonight?"

Fuzzy's ears turned red as he stepped on the gas and charged out of reach of the Jeep. "Guys from the soccer team," he explained to Winkie.

"They looked cold," she said sympathetically, reaching forward to turn the car heater up a notch.

Before long we had circled the block and were driving up through the alley into Feraci's lot. Fuzzy pulled his car in between a red Cadillac and a big blue Pontiac. Something about the Pontiac touched a troubling chord in my mind, but I couldn't remember what it was.

We got out and began moving toward the door, Mark and I being careful to walk side by side. Bix trailed behind us, his hands in the pockets of his brown jacket. Keeping up the appearance that nothing was wrong between Mark and me was turning out to be more of a strain than I would have thought. We were walking side by side but we avoided looking at each other.

Mark opened the door for me and I stepped thankfully into the warmth of Feraci's. Inside, it was thronged with the usual crowd of kids. The sounds of an electric guitar at war with some drums came blasting from the jukebox.

When we stepped into the main room, I was almost woozy with the heat and noise and looked at the Tiffany lamp dangling over the salad bar with the blank eyes of someone in a trance. But some instinct for danger sifted out of the general noise the quiet words, "That's him. That's Bix that just came in."

Startled, I looked behind me, but Bix stood there in his flyer's jacket, surveying the room, checking out possible desirable booths. A waitress wearing a Santa Claus hat passed us with a laden tray.

"You Bix Bixby?" I heard someone say.

A guy wearing tan jeans and a cowboy hat had walked up to Bix. I noticed the guy's lips seemed twisted in a permanent sneer. He was shorter than average, which may have been why he wore the hat.

Bix's amber eyes settled on this cowboy character. "So?" he said.

"So, I hear you're pretty fast. How'd you like to prove it?" The guy smiled.

Bix's eyes shifted away from him again and sought the empty booth in the corner. "Not interested," he said. He began to head toward the booth.

The boy in the hat jumped over two steps until he stood directly in front of Bix. "Afraid you're not fast enough, huh?"

Bix, who was somewhat taller, looked down on the guy. "No," he said coolly, "and if you don't move in two seconds I'm going to have to step over your body, fella."

The level of noise in Feraci's had subsided considerably and I saw a couple of men in white aprons and Santa Claus hats begin to hurry from behind the pizza counter in our direction.

"If you want a race, I'll race you, cowboy," Mark said.

I looked at him aghast.

The men wearing the white aprons loomed beside us. "Outside, boys," said the one with the five-o'clock shadow. "Now." He jerked his thumb in the direction of the door.

"Sure thing, mister," said the boy in the cowboy hat, hooking his thumbs in the belt loops of his jeans. As he turned toward the door he shot Mark a predatory look. "Just name the place, tubby."

Red blotches were appearing on Mark's neck. "Old airport. In twenty minutes." Mark had turned and began walking toward the door. "Come on, Fuzzy. I gotta go get my car."

"What's going on?" Winkie whispered to me. "Does this mean we don't get any pizza?"

"I'll take you to get the car, Metcalf," said a thin boy in a green letter sweater who had stepped out of a dark corner.

"Jeez," muttered Fuzzy, shooting a helpless look at Winkie.

Mark and the boy in the green sweater departed without a backward glance.

Bix put both hands on my shoulders and began guiding me to the door. "Come on," he said.

"Come on, Winkie," Fuzzy echoed, grabbing her hand. "We gotta go."

"Not even any take-out pizza?" asked Winkie wistfully.

Evidently she had yet to learn that boys intent on affairs of honor can be grandly indifferent to everyday things like pizzas. And common sense.

When we got out to the parking lot, I saw the skinny boy's car shooting into the alley leaving a white trail of exhaust behind it. We jumped into Fuzzy's car. Behind us, I could see that Feraci's was emptying. Not much pizza would be eaten tonight. It looked as if everyone was heading out to the old airport.

Fuzzy turned into the alley and soon we burst from its darkness into the lights of Lakeside Avenue. I sat in the back seat with Bix, shivering. "Is Mark really going to race that guy, Bix?" I asked. "Why is he doing this?"

Bix was looking out the window as intently as if he were on some committee for judging the street's Christmas decorations. I couldn't see his face.

"It is dangerous, isn't it?" I said. I pushed my hands in my coat pocket and pressed myself back against the seat cushions, but I knew it was the cold feeling inside and not the weather that was making me shiver.

"He must be crazy," said Fuzzy. "Metcalf's never raced before, has he? And the way he babies that car, heck, he still drives it like he's breaking it in. He's got to be crazy. There's no way else to explain it."

"We've got to stop him!" I wailed.

Bix turned to look at me. "How are we going to stop him?"

I didn't answer. I couldn't think of any way. It certainly wasn't as if I had any influence with Mark anymore. I sat miserably in silence until we drove up to the old airport. Built in the days when the city fathers had dreams of regular air service to Hampstead, the airport had not been used for planes for at least a decade. It was kept mown because occasionally car rallies were held on the grounds, but the wire and post fence that outlined the broad perimeters of the place had fallen down in several places and when we drove in, Fuzzy's headlights, shining on the runway, revealed that grass had grown up between the runway's slabs of concrete.

Behind us, I could see the headlights of other cars as they streamed in. Cars began pulling up around us on the grass, their headlights, like ours, trained on the runway. I looked around me frantically. I couldn't believe everyone was gathering around as if this race were some ordinary spectator sport like football or tennis. The blue Pontiac drove past us and stopped at the foot of the runway. I knew it would be only a matter of minutes until Mark arrived in his car.

A tear tricked down my face leaving a cold trail on my cheek. I felt so helpless and I was not used to feeling helpless. It was always my instinct to try to fix things up when they were going wrong. There just had to be some way to stop this race before somebody got killed, I thought. My helpless feelings seemed to be swelling up inside me like a balloon until I felt I was going to scream.

"Fuzzy," I said suddenly. "Can I borrow your car just to drive it down the road to that convenience store?"

"Heck of a time to want a snack or something," Fuzzy grumbled.

"I'll be right back," I said. "I promise."

I caught the keys as he threw them to me, then I moved over close to Bix and spoke quietly. "Stall them," I said. "Do anything you can to gain some time. I'm going to call Mark's mother."

Bix stiffened. "I don't know, Katy."

"Do you want Mark to get killed or something? Do you?" I said urgently.

Without waiting for an answer, I got in Fuzzy's car and backed out between the massed cars that were now parked around us. Then I turned Fuzzy's car around and headed back to the road. As I reached the road, I passed Mark's blue Studebaker. I was sure he must recognize Fuzzy's car speeding away from the scene and wonder what was going on but I couldn't worry about that now.

A convenience store was two miles down the road where the airport road intersected with the highway. As soon as I got there, I jumped out and ran to the pay telephone that stood near the ice machine. I was so jittery I dropped my quarter, but I quickly retrieved it, dropped it in the phone slot and dialed Mark's number.

After three rings, Mark's mother picked up the phone. When I heard her voice my knees sagged with relief. "Mrs. Metcalf?" I said. In the rush of events I couldn't remember her new married name.

"Yes?" she said.

"This is Katy Callahan. I'm out at the old airport and listen, this is important—Mark is about to be in a drag race and I can't figure out any way to stop him."

"Did you say a drag race?" she asked in a faint voice.

"Yes. That's why he came back home to get his car. He's going to race this boy in a blue Pontiac. I don't see how he can back down now even if he wanted to. There must be hundreds of kids out here. How fast can you get here? Bix is going to try to stall them."

"I'm coming now," she said, and she abruptly hung up.

I looked at the phone in my hand with amazement. It was hard to believe I had really done this. But what else could I have done? I only hoped Mark's mother was going to be able to get there soon enough.

Feeling my heart pounding in my throat, I jumped got back into Fuzzy's car and drove back toward the airport. Even a mile away, I could see the glow of all the headlights fixed on the runway.

As I drove up to the crowd of cars parked at the base of the runway, I could see Mark's Studebaker and the cowboy's blue Pontiac lined up side by side on the concrete. Farther out I could see two figures walking on the runway, caught in the glare of all the car headlights. The big one in the gray sweatshirt had to be Mark and the other wore a cowboy hat. They were looking down at the concrete as they walked toward us, presumably checking for potholes.

Fuzzy, and Winkie and Bix were standing just where I had left them.

"I told them they had better walk the course," said Bix. "It was the only thing I could think of."

"But they'll be back in a few minutes," I said anxiously. "And I'm afraid Mark's mother won't be here yet."

"Well, next I'll tell them we have to line up the noses of the cars exactly. Then we'll have to look for something to use for a starting flag. Then I'll tell them we have to have observers at the finish line. I'll be one of the observers and I'll walk down there as slow as I can. That's all I can do, Katy."

"Well, she's coming," I said, my teeth chattering in the cold.

When the two boys finally returned from walking the course, someone was able to produce a red flag from his trunk right away, so we hadn't been able to gain much time that way. The guy who produced the flag was wearing a hat that said Horner's Building Supplies, so I suppose it was the sort of flag you put on pieces of lumber that stick out behind your car to warn other drivers not to get up too close to you. The guy in the Horner's hat, looking indecently cheerful, volunteered to stand between the cars and throw down the starting flag.

"Wait a minute," shouted Bix. "We've got to have observers at the finish line or how are we going to know who really wins if it turns out to be close?"

"It won't be close," sneered the cowboy.

However, in the end the cowboy from Silver Lake picked an observer from his own town to go down to the finish line with Bix to ensure impartiality. Bix and the other boy then began walking down to the finish line.

I had been turning my head every half second to look back at Airport Road and at last I saw a pair of headlights coming in our direction. The car looked big enough to be a station wagon, I thought. I only hoped it was Mark's mother.

Mark had begun walking toward his car. At that point Mark's mother's station wagon shot into the airport and pulled up behind the rest of the parked cars. Mrs. Metcalf jumped out of the wagon, not bothering to close her door, and began struggling to get through the parked cars to reach Mark. She obviously had not paused to get her coat before she left home because she was wearing only a black turtleneck shirt and tweed pants. I could see her white face seeming to float above the black shirt, her open mouth a dark hole.

"Mark!" she shrieked when she managed to get closer. "Don't you move!"

A few kids near me turned to look as they heard her voice. "Give me those car keys, young man," she screamed. "Give them to me this minute."

When Mark spotted her, he flushed angrily, strode to his car and slammed the door shut behind him. I heard him yell, "Get in, cowboy. Let's race."

Standing between the cars the boy holding the red flag looked a little confused as Mark's mother finally reached the Studebaker and tried to open the door. When she realized it was locked she banged on the car door with her fist, screaming, "Mark! Open this door!" The wind ruffled her short hair as the car engines roared and the boy with the flag, darting an anxious glance to either side of him, brought down the flag.

I could hear Mark's mother's screaming over the roar of the engines as the two cars sped down the runway. The end of the runway was so far away our headlights didn't light it, but two cars had driven way out in the field to shine their headlights on the finish line. Out there I could make out a dark figure in front of one of the car's headlights that I knew must be Bix. With a quick intake of breath, I prayed that the two cars wildly careering down the runway wouldn't run down Bix at the finish line. He stepped out of the way of the headlights as the cars drew closer to the end of the runway and I couldn't see him anymore. Then suddenly Mark's Studebaker veered, skidded off the edge of the runway and flipped over. It all happened so fast, I hardly saw what happened, but there was Mark's car on its back, its wheels still spinning, with the lights of the cars at the finish line shining palely on it.

All the kids began to surge down the runway. I was afraid that I would remember this moment for the rest of my life as Mark's mother screamed behind me and I ran with the rest of kids toward the wrecked car.

By the time all of us reached Mark's car, Bix had already kicked in a window and was dragging Mark out. The broken window glass lay like rough marbles all over the ground, glittering in the light of the headlights. Mark's car, except for being upside down and slightly flattened on top, looked the same as always, its carefully groomed finish seeming incongruously perfect in this scene of human chaos. I could see that Mark had his arm around Bix's neck and was leaning on him heavily. Fuzzy rushed forward to help, since Mark was too heavy for Bix to carry by himself and it was pretty obvious he was in shock.

I started to run back to the starting line and tell Mark's mother that he looked as if he weren't hurt, but just then I saw the flickering blue light of a police car, and behind it the flashing light of an ambulance.

I soon realized that I was not the only person who had spotted the approaching law. The boy in the cowboy hat got into his car and began driving off. He was skirting the runway, driving with his lights turned off in the hope of being less conspicuous. But when he turned to drive out of the airport, the police pulled their car right across his path and blocked him.

All of us were backing away from Mark's car now, expecting that it might burst into flames any minute, but it just lay there on its back, its engine running, looking like some well mannered car that had had the bad luck to fall into the hands of Toad of Toad Hall. The ambulance attendants were making Mark lie down on the stretcher. They strapped him on, covered him up, and began wheeling him over to the ambulance. After they shoved the stretcher into the ambulance, I saw Bix scrambling into the back. A moment later, it drove off.

When the ambulance pulled out of the airport, I saw that it was closely followed by a brown station wagon driven by one extremely hysterical mother.

Fuzzy put his arm around Winkie and the three of us began walking back to Fuzzy's car.

"He looked okay to me, didn't he to you?" I asked Fuzzy anxiously. "He wasn't bleeding or anything."

"Yeah, just shock, that's all," he said. "Could have been a lot worse."

I discovered that I was shivering again and plunged my hands into my coat pockets.

"What a scene!" said Fuzzy, shaking his head. "I nearly flipped when Mark's mother showed up. I wonder how she figured out what was going on?"

I looked at the ground, scuffed my shoe in the dry grass and said nothing. I was hoping Mark would never find out who had blown the whistle on him.

Chapter Nine

Checkpoint Station on Lakeside Will Curb Cruising read the headline of the local section of the paper.

The city council has voted to establish a checkpoint on Lakeside Avenue in an effort to control the practice of cruising by local teens. The checkpoint, which will be at the corner of Mercer and Lakeside Avenue, will be in operation from five until midnight on Fridays and Saturdays and is designed to screen all cars. Any vehicle passing the checkpoint more than three times in an evening will be subject to a fine of thirty-five dollars.

Councilman Ben Fuller stated that the city council decided to take this measure because of concern expressed by Police Chief Carl Parsons about recent incidents of drag racing, vandalism, fist fights and unruly behavior. Chief Parsons reported that Saturday police were called to a drag race at the old airport on Airport Road at which two juveniles were charged with careless and reckless driving. One of the juveniles was treated at Hampstead General Hospital and released. Chief Parsons stated that this was the second incident of drag racing in the city in six months and it was his belief that these incidents were related to the cruising that occurs weekends on Lakeside.

Residents of West Side Village, a residential neighborhood contiguous to the Lakeside area, also presented a petition to the council protesting the noise and litter caused by cars of cruising teenagers.

I folded the morning paper and laid it aside. "That's torn it," I muttered.

"Hurry up, Katy," Mom said. "You'll miss the school bus."

I took a last sip of my hot chocolate and reached for my coat. Outside a horn blared. Startled, I pulled the curtains of the kitchen door aside and looked out to see Bix's car at the curb.

"Bye, Mom!" I called. Grabbing my books, I ran out to him.

He leaned over the seat and threw the door open for me. "Need a ride, lady?" He grinned.

I got in and tossed my books on the back seat. "This is luxury," I exclaimed. "A heater, even!" The school bus was heated only by the tightly packed bodies of the people who rode on it. I looked at him. "What's wrong?"

"What makes you think something's wrong?"

"I just wondered if you came by to pick me up in order to cheer me up a little or something. Have you talked to Mark? How is he?"

"Not too good. I went with him to the hospital, you know. His mother showed up there right on the heels of the ambulance and I swear she was worse off than he was. She kept bursting into tears and calling him her baby and telling him he ought to be grateful to you for trying to save his life."

"You wanted to tell me he knows I called her. That's why you came by."

His eyes flickered to my face. "Yup. You'll probably want to stay out of his way for a while. I tell you, Katy, he's in bad shape. His mom didn't just take his keys away from him, she's had the wheels of his car taken off. I went by there yesterday and it was up on blocks in the garage. She's not taking any more chances."

I sighed. "I did the wrong thing to call her, didn't I?"

"I'm not saying that. It turned out it didn't work, but that's not to say it was the wrong thing."

"I guess he'll never speak to me again."

Silence from Bix. He obviously did not feel very optimistic on that point himself.

"I was afraid he would get himself killed," I said.

"It was close enough. Lucky thing he happened to buckle his seat belt before he took off. It must have been a habit because he was so mad I don't think he knew what he was doing." Bix shook his head. "It's so stupid to get in a car when you're coming apart at the seams. Stands to reason you can't really drive when you're in that shape."

"I guess you saw the story in the paper about the police cracking down on cruising."

He grimaced. "Yeah. Just another nail in Mark's coffin, right? There's bound to be some strong feeling when it hits people that it was his race that triggered it."

"I'm really worried about him, Bix. I wish there was something we could do."

"Now, wait a minute," said Bix, looking at me warily.

"Don't worry," I said, managing to smile. "I'm not going to try to do anything. No plots. No plans. I'll stand clear."

"Good," said Bix. "Because it's his war, Katy. We can't do anything to make it better and we just might make it worse."

Bix drove the car into the traffic snarl that was the juniors' parking lot and found a space. He pulled sharply up on the parking brake. "Want to drive over to Silver Lake to that car show this afternoon?" he asked.

I reached for the door handle. "Don't think you have to cheer me up, Bix. I'm okay."

"Hey," he said. "Did you ever think that maybe it's me that could stand some cheering up? Fuzzy's flaked out on me. He wants to go everywhere now with that girl of his, the one with the braid and the weird name."

"Well, okay, then. Unless Mr. Hatchard slams us with a bunch of algebra homework, I'll go."

I didn't inquire why Celia wasn't going. Even if the two of them had made up, I knew that Celia wouldn't have gone to a car show. She didn't have time for trivialities.

When I passed the lockers on my way to homeroom a bunch of kids were gathered there talking. I don't think it was just my imagination that they seemed to turn their heads to look at me as I went by.

I have never wanted to find myself featured in the gossip mills of Hampstead High and I felt a momentary surge of anger at Mark for bringing it on me. As the girlfriend—or ex-girlfriend—of the guy who had singlehandedly put an end to the cruising down Lakeside, people would be pointing me out all day. Only sixteen years old and already I was notorious.

When I slid into my seat in homeroom, the bell still hadn't rung. Stacy Bolling leaned over in my direction and said, "How's Mark? I noticed he wasn't in school yesterday. Was he hurt in that race?"

I blinked rapidly. I hadn't thought about how people would be asking me about Mark. I realized suddenly that it wasn't going to be practical to act as if all was well between the two of us since it was pretty much a sure thing Mark would cut me dead the next time he saw me.

"I guess he was pretty shaken up," I said cautiously.

"Did they take his license away?"

"Gee, I don't know. I haven't talked to him."

"You haven't *talked* to him? I thought you two were going together?"

I shrugged my shoulders. "You know how people drift apart, Stacy." I did my best to look like a woman of the world for whom drifting apart was a common, even a boring event.

To my relief the bell rang then and people began pouring into the classroom.

"It's unconstitutional. That's what I say," a tall boy said as he passed me.

"My dad says they can regulate traffic anyway they want. He said if they want they could slap a six o'clock curfew on anybody under eighteen," said Mickey O'Rork.

"Hey! Wait a minute!" said the tall boy, obviously appalled by the idea of a six o'clock curfew.

"It's that dumb race," Linda Myerson put in as she took her seat. "None of this would have happened if those boys hadn't been so stupid."

"Don't look at me," said Tommy Vining. "I didn't have anything to do with it."

I pretended to be frantically studying chemistry, jotting notes in my notebook. The last thing I wanted was for somebody to wonder why I wasn't defending Mark. And why wasn't I defending Mark? I asked myself as I frantically wrote meaningless chemistry formulas on a sheet of notebook paper. It was true that I knew Mark didn't want his personal problems talked about all over school. And I knew it was no good my telling everybody that he had a lot on his mind. Everybody would want to know *what* was on his mind. And the chances are they wouldn't think whatever it was justified the crazy way he was behaving. But I recognized that wasn't the only reason I wasn't defending him. The fact is, I was kind of mad at him myself. I suppose you can only go on for so long making allowances for somebody and then you find yourself wishing they'd emigrate to Australia or something and quit ruining your life.

It was a very long day. All anyone talked about was the new anticruising ordinance. This was hardly surprising since the new ordinance would mean the end of social life as we knew it at our school. To judge from the tone of the remarks I overheard, an uprising of the peasants was in the making.

Everybody was against the new ordinance—the strange kids who shaved their heads and put bones through their earlobes, the straight kids who planned to join the army on graduation—all spoke as one voice against this affront to individual liberty. I wasn't surprised that Mark had decided to stay out of school on this particular day. It was the smartest thing I had seen him do in weeks.

After school, Bix gave me a ride home so I could check with Mom about driving with him over to the auto show. I felt deep relief as we drove away from the school.

"Long day, huh?" Bix said as we crested the hill.

"I feel years older," I said. "I guess that must be what suffering does to a person."

"Mark must look a hundred by now, then."

I felt a pang of guilt that I had forgotten all about what Mark must be going through.

"Poor Mark," I said contritely.

When we got to my house, I ran in and changed and told Mom where we were going.

"Will you be back by suppertime?" she asked.

"I don't know, Mom. We may just grab a bite at the mall over there. Don't hold supper for me."

I pulled a brush quickly through my hair and ran out again to the car.

It was a cold day, but the sun was shining and the sky, very smooth and high, was robin's-egg blue. It suddenly seemed possible that I could step into Bix's magic coach and leave my troubles behind. Life goes on, I found myself thinking. It's been rough, but I'll live. I may take up transcendental meditation, learn to knit, develop an interest in car shows. I opened the car door and got in.

"I told Mom I wasn't sure about supper, in case we wanted to get something to eat over there. Is there a place to grab a bite to eat at the Silver Lake Mall?"

"Bound to be," said Bix, taking off with a screech of tires.

"Slower," I suggested.

He grinned and the needle on the speedometer slowly dropped.

"Bix, why was that guy from Silver Lake looking for you? Have you ever done any racing?"

He rubbed his nose and looked embarrassed. "Well, after I fixed up this car, you know, and added a few things of my own, I was sort of curious to see what she'd do."

"So you raced somebody?"

"Yeah. The guy was driving a straight-off-the-rack '80 Chevy and I beat him pretty handily. Got her up to 130," he reported with ill-concealed pride. "But the takeoff was the thing that decided it. Fuzzy timed me and he said she did the first quarter mile in fifteen seconds."

"Wasn't that *dumb*, though?" I said. "Driving that fast?"

"Yeah, I decided that it was. That's why I haven't tried it again. The thing is, if you're under eighteen they can yank your license in this state just for breathing too hard. They don't even have to wait until you get the regular number of points on it. I started thinking I'd be crazy to risk that. I was right, too. Look at poor Mark."

"Did they yank his license?"

"I didn't ask. Seemed kind of tactless. The question's sort of academic now, anyway, isn't it? I mean, talk about literally no wheels."

"Awful," I agreed perfunctorily. I was thinking that I would rather see Mark with no wheels than dead. "I'm really glad you don't race," I said, "because I don't have any friends to spare these days."

He smiled at me. Unlike some ash blondes, who tend to look washed out, Bix had dark eyelashes so long that at times they seemed almost to cast his amber eyes in shade. Knowing him so well, I hardly ever looked at him anymore just to *look*. But when I did, he could still knock me out. I found myself catching my breath sharply.

"What's the matter?" he asked.

"Nothing," I said. "I was just—thinking."

What I was thinking was that it was amazing that Celia could suspect him of lying. You could imagine Bix being arrested for assault, but perjury—no. Lying was not his style at all.

The best word for Bix, I decided, was the old-fashioned word "true." You said it about a blade that was pure and straight, or a line that was unswerving, or a lover who would not cheat and it described Bix perfectly. He had his faults—not only was he likely to knock somebody flat on provocation any reasonable person would laugh at, but he could show a casual indifference to other people's comfort. For example, it would be a mistake to expect Bix to notice that you were about to faint from hunger. It wasn't the perfection of his character that made me think of him as true, but rather the way he was always so perfectly who he was, the way he rarely deviated from his own slightly savage code.

"Private thoughts?" asked Bix.

I shrugged. "So the show is actually at the Silver Lake Mall?"

"Right. Restored cars."

It was only about a twenty-minute drive to the nearby town of Silver Lake so it wasn't long before we were driving up to the mall where the marquee announced Antique Car Display.

Inside the mall, parked at close intervals along its length was an array of elderly cars which had been rebuilt and repainted until they looked better than any of the new cars parked in the lot outside. I recognized that behind these cars was the same fanaticism that had driven Mark to restore his old Studebaker to its pristine glory. He was chasing down parts and ordering esoteric gear from car magazines before he had even passed his driver's test.

A gleaming Model A stood next to an Edsel. The Edsel had a fierce printed sign on its windshield, Treat this as you would another man's wife. Look but don't touch. The Model A took a more low key tack, Please

Do Not Touch. It was easy to see why the caution was necessary because the finishes were as smooth as mother of pearl and seemed to positively cry out Touch Me.

"Nice, huh?" said Bix. "Too bad that—well, you know."

Too bad, I suppose he meant, that Mark was incommunicado and not up to coming because this show would have been absolutely and completely his cup of tea.

"I bet it would be better at night," Bix said a bit wistfully, "when some of the owners hang around and you could ask them questions."

"It's nice now, too," I said. "They're beautiful cars."

"Yeah." He smiled. "They are, aren't they? You hungry yet?"

"What did you say?"

"I said do you want to grab a bite to eat yet?"

It was hard to believe. Bix was actually thinking about my comfort and there in the presence of all those luscious automobiles, too.

"I could stand to get something to eat," I said. I decided I had better snap up this offer because I couldn't count on him thinking of it again. If one of the owners came along and he and Bix started talking about torques and compression I would have to go off and eat by myself.

We settled on hot dogs at a nearby snack shop, then went back for a dessert course of automobiles.

When we left the mall, it wasn't particularly late but night falls so early in December that we ended up driving home in total darkness. Only the light from the dash and the faint light reflected back from the headlights on the road shed any illumination in the car. The greenish light of the radio and the speedometer painted a faint line along Bix's profile and an indirect glow showed the suggestion of the modeling of his jaw and his cheekbone.

The heater was sending out warm air and making my legs warm and my shoes hot. Maybe because it had been such a trying day I found myself growing drowsy. Bix stretched out one arm on the seat behind me and I found myself wanting to sort of snuggle up to the hollow of his arm and rest my head on his shoulder.

"I hope this isn't carbon monoxide poisoning," I said, shaking my head and pulling myself awake with an effort.

He looked at me indulgently. "Can't be," he said. "I'm wide awake. Nice, wasn't it? Not a hundred cars, but the ones that were there were very choice."

"Nice," I said, yawning. I was so sleepy that I finally let myself sink back against Bix's outstretched arm. It was a very odd feeling, this feeling of being magnetically drawn to Bix, but I was really too sleepy to worry about it. I would think about it later.

"Wake up, Katy. We're home," said Bix's voice suddenly.

I opened my eyes, and realized that I was leaning right up against Bix. I could feel the roughness of sweater on my cheek. I straightened up, glad it was dark so that he couldn't see me blushing. I was even more glad Celia wasn't there watching.

"Golly, I fell asleep," I said.

"Can you make it up to the door or do you want me to walk up there with you?"

"Oh, I can walk. I was just a little sleepy." I yawned again.

"Funny thing," he said. "Car shows don't do that to me."

"A long day," I murmured. I threw the car door open and was hit by a rush of icy air that woke me up instantly and set me shivering. "See you," I said. I made a run for my front door.

Bix, I was thinking as I ran breathlessly up to the door. How odd to be snuggling up against Bix. But nice.

Chapter Ten

A couple of days later I woke up with a fever and sore throat. Aha! I thought, examining the silver line of mercury that stopped at 101. My unconscious realized that the dance is the day after tomorrow and it has given an open invitation to all passing viruses.

"Katy!" called Mom. "Aren't you up, yet? You're going to be late for school."

"I'm sick," I said, confirming this with a prompt sneeze.

I stayed home from school and spent the rest of the day watching game shows and soap operas and filling a wastebasket with crumbled tissues.

"Tell me, Donna," said the handsome face on the

television screen, "is it my baby? I have the right to know."

"Leave me alone!" Donna cried. "How can you come to me like this after deserting me the way you did? You have no hold on me anymore. I'm beginning a new life with Robin. He is gentle and caring, everything you never were. Get out of here, Max, or I'm warning you, I'll call Daddy."

Donna reached for the phone, but Max, the cad, knocked it out of her hands. Tears were streaming from Donna's eyes, beautiful tears that streamed down her high cheekbones.

"You think I'm afraid of your father, don't you?" said Max, his nostrils flaring. "Let me tell you, all the money the Flemings have can't buy Max Stoddard."

"You killed Melinda, didn't you?" cried Donna. "You killed her! It wasn't Tom after all."

"Katy," Mom called from the kitchen. "Telephone."

I sighed and snapped off the set. Since this was my first day out sick, I was pretty hazy on who Donna and Max were, much less Melinda and Tom, so it was no great loss to go to the phone.

But why, I wondered sadly, couldn't life be more like a soap opera? People had such lovely, shouting scenes in soap operas. Nobody ever bottled his feelings up. If life were like soap operas, Mark would have come storming over to the house and accused me of playing around behind his back with Bix. Then he would have shouted at me for telling his mother he was drag racing and would have concluded by saying he wouldn't take me to the Christmas dance on a bet. I would have wept pretty tears that didn't smear my mascara, and would have cried that I had only been trying to save his life and would have wound up by saying I wouldn't go to the Christmas dance with him if he were the last boy on earth. He would storm out, slamming the door and I would cry some more, and a good time would be had by all.

Unfortunately, in real life, it seemed, things didn't happen like that at all. Since the race, Mark was just not around much anymore. He had been back in school since Tuesday, but I think he was eating lunch with Denise. I saw them come out of the cafeteria line together. When Mark and I saw each other in Algebra or Latin he was always as polite to me as he would have been to one of his mother's friends. It was kind of chilling. Of course, the result was exactly the same as if we had had one of those splendid shouting matches that they had on the soap operas. I knew exactly where I stood. At ground zero. Blown away.

It's just that there was something unsatisfyingly incomplete about the real life method. Since our date for the Christmas dance had never been officially canceled—breaking a date presents certain technical difficulties when people are barely speaking—I was haunted by the fear that Mark would show up Saturday night with a boutonniere in his lapel and act astonished that I was wearing an apron and busy cleaning out the oven.

I had no desire whatever to go to the Christmas dance, but it would have been nice to have that loose end tied up. Luckily, my cold neatly solved my problem. Nobody could expect me to go to a dance when I was sick.

I wobbled into the kitchen and picked up the phone. "Hullo?"

"Katy, it's Bix. Are you sick or something?"

"Yup, a fever of 101 this mording," I reported proudly. "Dough fever dow, but then you can't expect be to keep up that kind of perforbance indefinitely. Id's a code."

"I sort of guessed that. How about I bring you over some hot chicken soup?"

"You bust be kidding."

"No kidding. My mom's just made gallons of it. Supposed to be just the trick for colds."

"Oh, you don't have to do that," I said, catching a glimpse of my flyaway hair in my reflection off the oven door.

"No trouble. Be there in a few minutes."

I dropped the phone. "It's Bix," I said to Mom. "He's cubbing over."

Sneezing, I dashed back to my bedroom and began working frantically to bring my hair and face up to their usual standard. Having done what I could with that, I stashed my shabby bathrobe in the laundry hamper and borrowed the nice new quilted number the family had got Mom for her birthday. By the time the doorbell rang, I had some hope that I looked like Camille and not like an ad for Nyquil.

Mom answered the door while I arranged the folds of the quilt around me and gracefully reclined on my bed. I heard Mom thanking Bix for the soup and promising to feed it to me for supper, then he strode into the room.

"You look terrible," he said.

"I ab sick," I said with dignity.

"Well, don't breathe on me," he said. "Do you need me to bring you anything from school?"

"Dough thanks. I have all my books."

"Drink orange juice, take vitamin C. Get over this thing. I'm lonely. I don't have anybody to talk to anymore. Fuzzy's always off with that girl of his now and Mark—"

"I know all about Mark," I said. "Off playing kitcheekitchee koo with Denise. It doesn't bother bee a bit. I ab over it. I plan to take up transcendental meditation and achieve idder peace."

Bix smiled a crooked smile. "Good. I better go or the next thing you know I'll be catching it from you."

"Dodsense," I said. "Whad germ would dare?" I sneezed.

Bix bid me a hasty farewell and fled the virulent viruses that filled my room.

I blew my nose. Bix was lonely? What about Celia? Where was she?

* * *

I had a record short-term, three-day cold. While this underlined the psychological nature of my ailment, it meant that I was actually hale and hearty by Saturday night, the night of the Christmas dance. I decided this did not really matter. Since I had already missed two days of school, in the eyes of the world I was officially sick and, even though I hadn't yet begun with the transcendental meditation, I could at least feel the kind of inner peace that came from the assurance that Mark would not show up on my doorstep wearing a boutonniere.

When the phone rang, however, I jumped a mile. I picked it up gingerly. "Hello?" I said.

"Katy? It's Bix. Say 'murmuring.'"

"Murmuring?"

"You're cured. Let's go for a drive. I'm stir crazy."

"But they've got that checkpoint on Lakeside now."

"There are other roads. Aren't you sick of sitting around there staring at four walls?"

Now that he mentioned it, I was. "Maybe we could drive around and look at the Christmas decorations," I said.

"Okay. Pick you up in ten minutes."

Minutes later in my room, I was pulling on black leggings and reaching for my big sweater with the red and green squiggles on it when I suddenly thought—where is Celia? I knew she didn't have time for much social life, but didn't she even want to go to the

Christmas dance? Probably some sort of flute commitment interfered, I decided, as I slipped my shoes on. I knew that Celia didn't let anything come between her and her ambition to be a first-class flutist.

I peeked in on Mom and Dad. They were snuggled into bed under the covers watching a sad movie on the VCR.

"I'm going driving with Bix," I said.

"When will you be back?" asked Mom, wiping the tears from her face.

"Oh, I don't know. We're going to look at Christmas decorations and stuff."

"Shh," said Mom. Someone seemed to be in the process of dying on the film.

I tiptoed out of the room and a moment later I heard Bix's horn.

I ran outside. When I slid over into the front seat, the warm darkness of the car slid over me like an envelope. There is something self-contained about a car in the wintertime. It was a little world of its own. And tonight just Bix and me in it. In a way that I would not have cared to confess to Celia, I liked that.

"You want Christmas decorations?" said Bix. "We could drive around West Side Village."

West Side had quite a few lighted Santas up on chimneys, plywood snowmen with floodlights trained on them, electric candles placed one per window and colored lights wound around arbor vitae bushes.

"Wasn't this one of those neighborhoods that complained about the litter and vandalism from kids cruising on Lakeside? I never heard about any vandalism? Where did they get that idea?"

"Probably made it up," said Bix cynically. "Some people just don't want anybody to have fun."

We then swung by the living nativity scene one of the churches had put up. It had a real donkey and a couple of real sheep in a fenced enclosure near a manger scene.

Next, for old times' sake, we drove once down Lakeside Avenue, past the checkpoint.

"I think we've seen most of it," said Bix when we turned off onto Trembull. "Ready to go home? Or do you want to drive some more?"

"Drive some more," I said promptly. I leaned back against the seat and worked on resisting the temptation to move over closer to Bix. I watched his hands on the steering wheel. They were large for his wrist and the knuckles had a couple of scabs on them. Could it really be less than two weeks ago that Bix and Mark were having that fight? I thought wonderingly. It seemed like aeons ago.

We were driving through the Baker Heights subdivision and suddenly I realized we were going right past Mark's house. The lights were on in the garage and I could see his blue Studebaker, still slightly caved in on top, sitting up on what looked like concrete blocks.

I couldn't help recoiling when I saw it. I could imagine the pain it must cause Mark to see his beloved car sitting there stranded, like a beached whale.

Bix followed my glance and drew his brows together. I supposed only force of habit had brought him in this direction. He certainly hadn't intended for me to start thinking about Mark.

"I'm worried about Mark," I said. "He's so unhappy, I'm afraid he might do something desperate."

"He already has done something desperate," said Bix. "That's what got him in so much trouble."

"But now he must be even more unhappy. What if he does something like—oh, run away with Denise! You know, the way they were talking about."

Bix shot me a questioning look. "Would you care?"

"Well," I said, "I wouldn't enjoy seeing him wreck his whole life, if that's what you mean. It's hard to give up on your friends. Well, heck, Bix, look at Celia. She's given you plenty of grief, and you haven't given up on her."

"Wrong!" said Bix, turning onto a two-lane highway. "I've given up on her."

"What!" I said.

"Given up. G-I-V-E—"

"I can spell it," I interrupted him. "What happened?"

Bix was driving out onto the dark country roads I remembered so well from when he used to set out with me to pour out his troubles about Celia. I supposed they were kind of his "thinking roads," the ones he turned to naturally when he wanted a long vacant stretch of road on which to sort things out in his own mind.

"For one thing, we were supposed to be going together," he said, "but I felt like she saw me less often than her dentist. It was as if she only wanted to see me when she didn't have anything better to do."

"The flute is a very demanding instrument," I said.

"Stop it! I don't want to hear anymore about the flute. I've heard enough about the flute already. And do you know she never did believe what I told her about our trip to the beach? What's her problem? I started asking myself. She actually accused me of plotting and planning all the time to get some way to be alone with you."

"Sounds like she's losing her grip on reality," I said sympathetically.

Bix grinned. "Well, I wouldn't go that far," he said.

"Maybe not actually psychotic," I amended.

"It's like she's always pushing me away, do you know what I mean?"

"So you two are really kaput?" I said, inching over a little closer to him so as to hear better.

"Finished," he said. "I still like Celia, but it's like she's living in another state."

"I know just what you mean!" I said, with a sudden shock of recognition. "That's the way I feel about Mark. I have a—a respect for him, you know. But it's kind of a distant feeling because he's just not there. It's as if he's gone away."

We were slowing down, which caught my attention because when driving, Bix was much more likely to speed up than to slow down. Finally he pulled off onto the shoulder. We were obviously out in the middle of nowhere. There were no lights but those of the car as far as I could see. I knew we must be near the plowed fields of his uncle's farm where he had once taught me how to drive. He turned off the headlights but left on the parking light.

"Katy," he said, "if I—well, you wouldn't push me away, would you?"

I shook my head silently. His eyes were cast in shadow when he turned toward me, but the faint light traced his jaw and skated lightly over the edges of his fair hair. He lifted a battered hand and touched my lips with his finger, then bent his head and kissed me.

It was strangely unlike the kiss we had staged in front of Celia's chemistry class. This was a soft kiss that made me want to melt against him and kiss him again. He put his hands on my shoulders and drew me closer and we kissed again. It was so right, I wondered why we hadn't done it before. Lifetimes have been spent in worse ways than kissing Bix.

Though we usually had so much to say to each other, we had quit talking altogether. I raised my finger and I traced the outline of his face, his eyes, his nose and he laughed. How I liked Bix, I thought. How right he was for me. He ruffled my hair with his fingers and kissed my forehead. Nice, I thought. Let's do it again.

"We'd better go," Bix said after a while. "We don't want the Highway Patrol coming along thinking we're a disabled car."

Certainly not, I thought, suddenly sitting up straight.

He started up the engine and turned the car around. I realized then that the car had grown cold without my realizing it. Now the engine started pumping out heat once more and the windows started to haze over so I had to take out a handkerchief and wipe off the inside of the windshield. Once the windshield was clear, I rested my head on Bix's shoulder and he put his arm around me. It seemed to belong there.

When we pulled up at the curb in front of my house, yellow light was shining in squares through the living-room curtains. Bix opened the car door for me and I stepped outside. It was a cold night but very clear, with tiny stars pulsing as if they had come alive. With an odd sense of detachment, I heard our footsteps on the concrete of the walk as we walked up to the front door. Everything seemed very far away except for Bix. I wasn't thinking anything much except that I wanted to kiss him again.

"You remember when Celia said I was always looking for ways to be alone with you?" Bix asked.

"Uh-huh?"

"I think maybe she was right," he said, his eyes crinkling at the corners.

It was reassuring somehow that our good-night kiss on the front steps was a practical, everyday sort of kiss, unlike the soft kisses in the car. Still friends, I thought happily.

After New Year's, Fuzzy and Winkie and Bix and I all went out to the mall with bags full of things that were the wrong color or size that we were supposed to return for our families. The mall seemed to be full of people who were there on precisely the same errand. A good many of the things people were returning seemed to be stuffed into crumpled grocery bags instead of the proper bags they had come in. And judging by the set look around people's lips, a good many of the necessary receipts had been misplaced as well.

"It's the Christmas rush in reverse," said Winkie.

"Yeah, but for this nobody's smiling," Fuzzy pointed out.

"I am," said Bix cheerfuly.

I wasn't. I had just looked over into the pet shop and caught sight of Mark and Denise. They were standing in front of the puppy cages looking at each other with a strange intensity.

Bix followed my glance, then looked at me doubtfully.

"There's something sick about it," I said. "I can't help it."

"Maybe you miss him?" suggested Bix.

"I guess I do," I said, frowning. "But not the way you think."

He put his arm around me. "Hey, that's okay, Katy. I miss him, too."

Winkie and Fuzzy had walked ahead to the fountain and Winkie was standing at the edge of it, holding a coin. "I'm making a wish!" she called. "Come on, you guys, let's all make a wish."

Bix and I moved along to join them at the fountain. I watched Winkie's coin arch over the water and hit with a small spash.

"Old Druid rite, my dad tells me," commented Bix.

I was already reaching in the change purse of my wallet for a dime. I found a new one, which seemed a good sign. It wouldn't have all its wishes used up. I saw that Bix had dug up a dime, too. He looked at me quizzically and we tossed them into the fountain. The twin dimes arched over the water, winking in the light, then hit, each of them sending up a small umbrella of water as it struck, and then sliding slowly under the water.

"I think he may come back," he whispered in my ear.

I reached blindly for his hand. I wondered why it had taken me so long to realize that I loved Bix.

* * * * *

COMING NEXT MONTH!
#5 Hart Mystery
ROBIN'S REWARD
by Nicole Hart

The youngest member of the Adirondacks gang now is involved in a big mystery and a little romance!

"We sure got our adventure!" Robin exclaimed.

"Did you have fun?" Eustice's eyes behind his glasses were gentle and large.

"So much fun! I'd like to have another one before the summer ends!"

She saw him smile and felt his hands in her curls. They tightened to pull her head back so that he could look more fully into her face.

"About that reward..." he began.

"Ouch! You're pulling my hair!"

"Sorry." His voice was soft.

Robin met his gaze, and instinctively her hand moved up to his shoulder.

Eustice cleared his throat. "I've never kissed a girl and I'm not sure I'm going to do it right," he said. "Does that bother you?"

"Why should it?"

His face became a blur as he moved closer. She shut her eyes and felt his lips touch hers with a firm, insistent pressure.

COMING NEXT MONTH
FROM
CROSSWINDS™

A KINDRED SPIRIT
by Ann Gabhart

A sensitive young artist becomes aware of a dark family secret. A luminous story that transcends the bounds of everyday life.

THE RIGHT MOVES
by M.K. Kauffman

Why was Brad troubled by doubts when K.C. launched himself into his latest crusade? Did he fear the truth—or the consequences?

AVAILABLE THIS MONTH

SHOCK EFFECT
Glen Ebisch

KALEIDOSCOPE
Candice Ransom